M21100

THIS BOOK IS THE PROPERTY OF THE
Georgia State Board of Education
AND IS FURNISHED TO
Miller County Library

JAMES S. PETERS, Chairman
CLAUDE PURCELL, State Supt. of Schools

SOUTHWEST GEORGIA REGIONAL LIBRARY
DECATUR - MILLER - SEMINOLE COUNTIES
BAINBRIDGE, GEORGIA

SO-BCO-622

TREASURE OF ACAPULCO

TREASURE OF ACAPULCO

by

Dorothy Witton

Julian Messner, Inc.   **New York**

Published by Julian Messner, Inc.
8 West 40 Street, New York 18

Published simultaneously in Canada
by The Copp Clark Publishing Co. Limited

© Copyright 1963 by Dorothy Witton

Printed in the United States of America

Library of Congress Catalog Card No. 63-7359

For all of my Acapulco friends
and for Thully

Contents

TREASURE OF ACAPULCO

1

Summons From Uncle Juan

DAWN FILTERED SLOWLY INTO ACAPULCO, SPREADING A
pale sheen over the bowl of the town and the crescent-
shaped bay. Roosters crowed lustily. Insistent bells
clanged from the big church on the plaza.

Tony Castillo stepped out of one of the small houses
on the slope above the bay and drew a deep-chested
breath of early morning coolness. His hair was still sleep
rumpled, but his black eyes were wide awake and eager.
This was the time of day he liked best.

He watched eagerly as the sunrise exploded over the
eastern mountains. Perched on the Mexican hilltops, the
luxurious tourist hotels emerged in the growing light like
fantastic palaces. But in the foothills below, near the
edge of the sea, the coast people lived very much as they
always had, in adobe houses of pastel colors, bordering
worn footpaths which led to the docks.

The light grew until it flooded the sky, made a silver
mirror of the bay and finally crept into the palm-shaded
patios.

It was November. The humid months of the rainy
season were over. From now until April the skies would

11

be cloudless, each day more perfect than the last. Except for a few more weeks at school, time stretched luxuriously ahead of Tony—time to fish, to dive into the depths of bay and ocean, to lie on the golden beaches.

The years of obedience to his uncle were almost over, he thought to himself with satisfaction. From now on, surely, at almost sixteen, he would be allowed to live life the way he wanted to—the way his fisherman father had lived it.

"Psst! Tony!" Aunt Raquel's ample figure appeared in the doorway behind him. "Here's the money for the fish. Tell Don Clemente I want *huachinango*—still wiggling! And hurry. Your uncle will be ready for breakfast soon."

"The idea of our buying fish," Tony muttered, "when we have a fisherman in the family. If I had a boat—"

"Yes, well, but you don't have," his aunt interrupted practically. "Run now!"

But I will have soon, Tony thought to himself, his bare feet slapping on the hard dirt path and then down a flight of cement steps to the coast boulevard and across that to the docks. There he stood for a moment, gazing thoughtfully at the fleet of fishing cruisers rocking in the light breeze.

*Some*day I'll have one of those, he told himself. But that day was probably rather distant. Those fancy fishing boats cost real money! In the meantime, a *canoa*—one of the dugouts the night fishermen used for smaller game—was more within the realms of possibility. Tony had decided to wait until New Year's to approach his uncle about a loan for a *canoa*. Perhaps the festive season of Christmas and the good business it brought to the small family grocery store would soften Uncle Juan's severity a little. . . .

"Tony!"

The boy wheeled quickly to see a lad of about his own age, also dressed in rolled-up denims and an open shirt with the tails tied loosely around his waist. In this he resembled most of the Acapulco boys. But in other respects he was different. Bright blue eyes seemed too large for the thin, sunburned face, and the blond hair was bleached almost white. Although the boys were almost the same height, Peter appeared frail in contrast to Tony, whose mahogany-brown body was well-muscled and robust.

"*Hola*, Pedro!" Tony grinned. "What brings you to the docks so early?"

"I was hoping I'd see you here." The boy smiled, a little shyly. "I wanted to tell you that I've got the promise of two aqualungs today. You remember you promised to teach me skin diving with a lung?"

"*Sí, hombre!*" Tony's black eyes sparkled. "I'll not only teach you—we'll find a lobster for dinner, if we're lucky! You come and eat it with us. If not lobster, then octopus in its own ink. Aunt Raquel cooks them—" He kissed the tips of his fingers in the Mexican gesture that meant a mouth-watering delicacy. "*Exquisito!*"

The blond boy laughed. "I don't know about the octopus," he said, making a face. "The lobster, yes!"

"You haven't tasted octopus yet?" Tony was shocked. "You don't know! Besides, it might put a little meat on that skeleton of yours." He tapped Peter's bony chest.

"Nothing seems to do that," the thin boy said lightly.

"But aren't the octopuses dangerous, Tony? I always thought—"

He stopped as Tony grinned broadly. "You always thought they were one of the awful monsters of the ocean, eh? I guess the poor octopus is one of the most slandered creatures in existence! Even the big ones are shy and get away from people as fast as they can. And the little ones we find here in the bay couldn't hurt you if they wanted to."

"I guess I have a lot to learn," Peter said.

"Well, you haven't been here very long yet." Tony's voice was kind. "Look, Pedro, why don't you come now and breakfast with us?" he added impulsively. "I'm down here buying fish—red snapper, right from the ocean into the frying pan."

"Sounds good." The other boy smiled. "But Dad's expecting me for breakfast in the pension. Thanks anyway, Tony. I'll see you about ten o'clock, then? On Caleta Beach, by the almond trees?"

"At ten." Tony nodded. *"Hasta luego!"*

He stood for a moment, watching the thin figure dart across the boulevard and up one of the side streets which were lined with inexpensive boardinghouses.

He is a nice boy, Tony thought tolerantly, even if he is a gringo. And I think he is a lonely boy.

At the beginning of the fall term, Pedro, whose name in English was Peter Carson, had registered in the high school which Tony attended. He was the only *Norteamericano* in the school and at first the Acapulco boys had given him a rough time. But Peter had quietly hung on, ignoring the jibes, being as friendly as they would allow him to be, but not pushing it. He spoke Spanish understandably though imperfectly, and he grinned readily when the boys laughed at his language mistakes. Gradually, they had accepted him. Three things had helped to overcome the natural standoffishness toward a "foreigner." One was Peter's obvious poverty; another was his good humor; but the clinching factor was his ability to draw caricatures. With pen, pencil or crayon, Peter could characterize his schoolmates and teachers in clever, exaggerated portraiture which gave him his turn to ridicule gently, and the naturally artistic Mexicans loved it.

Tony had been one of the first to make casual overtures of friendship. And walking home with the *huero*—the blond one—he had learned a few facts about him. Peter was here with his father, who had formerly been a newspaperman and was now writing a book. His mother was dead. The two Carsons had lived in Guadalajara for a year before coming to Acapulco in August. Peter loved the sea and he loved Acapulco and he yearned for a boat—all of which was enough to make him Tony's brother in spirit, foreigner or not!

As Tony trotted now to the fishermen's beach that curved out from one end of the docks, he wondered where the blond boy had gotten enough money to rent two aqualungs. But speculation about Peter faded to the back of his mind as he haggled good-naturedly with Don Clemente over the price of the fish which he delivered to his aunt a few minutes later.

"Still wiggling." He grinned at her.

"*You* didn't wiggle much, though," she retorted. "What

kept you? Your uncle wants to see you, Tony, before the store gets busy. He's in the office."

"I don't have to work in the store today?" Tony asked, alarmed. "You said yesterday that with the girls home—"

"No," Aunt Raquel replied calmly. "This is about something else, I think."

Afterward Tony wondered why, from that mild statement, he had felt a presentiment of disaster. There was nothing unusual about Uncle Juan wanting to see him. It could have concerned a hundred relatively unimportant things: his not-too-good record in school, a Saturday errand to be done, a mistake in the store accounts. . . .

But Tony felt, even as he walked slowly to the cubbyhole office at the back of the adjoining store, that it was not any of these. It was a big thing.

"You wanted to see me, *Tío?*" he asked from the door, looking at his uncle's pale lean face, with sharp amber-colored eyes which were now running over a column of figures, the thin lips moving as he checked them.

"Come in, Antonio, and close the door." Juan Gonzales leaned back in his chair and turned his penetrating eyes on Tony. "Sit down."

Tony's heart thumped. His uncle rarely called him Antonio. This was bad. He knew it was something bad, though his uncle's pale lips were smiling now.

Half prepared as he was, the blow was still staggering when it came. . . .

"We're moving to Mexico City at the end of January, Antonio. All of us." Uncle Juan's voice was complacent.

"I have a fair enough offer for this store and I'm going back to my small hotel business in the city. The girls will have better schooling and for you there's a fine hotel school where you can learn the business from experts."

Tony was stunned. He opened his mouth but no sound came out. His uncle was not looking at him. He was rolling a pencil in his fingers, the smile of satisfaction still on his face.

"Your school record is not startling, Tony, as you know, but you have managed to do well in English. And since you've been helping around the store, I have realized that you actually know more of the language than I thought. English is very important now, with more North Americans coming to Mexico every year. You're good at handling the customers, too. With the tourist business booming as it is, a career in a hotel is the ideal thing for you. You can work in our small place, perhaps as bellboy, while you learn the latest methods in this new hotel school. And then—"

"You mean—" Tony's incredulous voice was ragged and he cleared his throat. "You mean you want me to go with you to Mexico City and *never* come back to Acapulco?"

The anguish in his tone was so undisguised that his uncle really looked at him for the first time, startled.

"Ah yes, you're an Acapulqueño, aren't you?" he said after a moment, with dry sarcasm. "Well, perhaps in a few years, after you've learned the business thoroughly, you might find an opening here in Acapulco. I was hoping, however, that you'd want to carry on *my* hotel and stay with the family, at least until you marry."

Tony drew a long gasping breath, as though he had just emerged from a too-deep dive.

"Uncle Juan," he said slowly, trying to be calm and to choose his words carefully, "ever since you and Aunt Raquel first came to Acapulco and took my sister Marta and me into your family, I have done whatever you asked and tried to please you. I went to school. I worked at English. I helped in the store—when the other boys were out on the beaches and on the bay. I appreciated what you did for us, most of all for Marta's sake. But for me—all that time, I was thinking of the sea. Nothing but the sea! Waiting till I'd be old enough to be on my own so I could go back to my own work. My father was a coast fisherman. I was born to be a fisherman. I can't leave Acapulco. *This is my town—my home!* I wouldn't be any good in Mexico City. I wouldn't work out in the hotel business—ever!"

He paused for breath, seeing the gathering frown on his uncle's face but, for once, not heeding it. This was a matter of life and death to him and it had to be straightened out *now*.

"Take Marta, if you want," he added in a voice that was almost a whisper. "She likes the city. But I must stay here, where I belong."

The silence lengthened and grew ominous. Finally his uncle broke it.

"I suppose I should have expected this," he said with cold bitterness, "but somehow I thought you had given up long ago that childish idea about living from the sea. You know what I think of beach bums."

"Fishermen and skin divers are not beach bums!" Tony cried hotly. "My father was a fisherman and he made our living from the sea!"

Uncle Juan gave an almost imperceptible shrug. "I have no wish to criticize your father, Antonio. He was your Aunt Raquel's stepbrother and he was a good man, according to his own lights. But you must admit that the living he made was not very adequate. When your aunt and I came to Acapulco, after his death, you and Marta were penniless and hungry and in rags."

"He'd had bad luck for a while before that," Tony muttered defensively. "It had been a bad season—"

"It's always a bad season for small fishermen," his uncle interrupted shortly. "You can see that from looking around our own neighborhood here, where they live, and looking at the debts they owe on our books. Either there are too many storms or the fish are scarce or the price goes down. Always something! I want to see you established in a business that will pay you a decent salary, boy! Something stable that you can count on!"

"Eventually I planned to get a fishing cruiser," Tony said. "You just can't fail with that—tourist business or commercial fishing, on your own."

"You know what they cost?" his uncle asked relentlessly. "More money than you'll ever see, if you insist on making your living from the ocean!"

"I was going to ask you, after New Year's, to lend me the money for a *canoa*," Tony said, feeling his throat dry and scratchy. "I could pay it back in a couple of months and then begin saving for a launch."

His uncle looked at him for several minutes. When he spoke, there was a finality to his words that Tony knew from experience would brook no further appeal.

"I have told you my plans for you, Antonio. If you insist on trying it your own way, go ahead. *For three months.* If, by the end of January, when the family moves, you have saved a sizable amount toward a boat—with no assistance from me—then I'll say no more. You can stay here. If not, you will go with us to the city and follow the career I have chosen for you. Remember, I am your legal guardian and I can force you to come!"

Tony stared at him. "What do you call a 'sizable amount' toward a launch?" he asked cautiously.

"Not less than two thousand pesos," his uncle answered coolly.

Two thousand pesos! Tony gulped in despair. It was impossible. And Uncle Juan knew that it was impossible.

"You have the best time of the year to do it—no rain, lots of tourists," his uncle reminded him. "If you can't save that much now, you can't even make a living the rest of the year."

"But school—helping in the store—"

"The school term will be over in a few weeks. And I release you from all work in the store. From now on, *you're on your own,* for three months."

Implacably, he turned back to his figures. And after a moment, Tony stumbled out and walked through the patio with unseeing eyes.

2

Tony's Other World

"Tony!" His sister Marta's voice stopped him on the way to the street door. "Where have you been? Your breakfast is ready."

"I don't want any—" His eyes fell on the golden fried fish, the bowls of red and green chile. A moment before, he would have sworn he couldn't swallow a mouthful but the sight and smell of the appetizing food was too much for him. He slumped at the veranda table and picked up a tortilla.

"What's the matter?" Marta asked sympathetically. "Did Uncle Juan scold you for something?"

"Not exactly." He patted her hand. "I'll tell you later, *chiquita.*"

He was very fond of his sister but he didn't feel like discussing this proposed move to the city with her right now. She would probably be pleased by the change. She was ambitious—though not in the way Uncle Juan was. She wanted to be a teacher and Tony was proud of her aspirations. For that reason, if for no other, he wanted to do nothing that would antagonize Uncle Juan.

But as he ate the fish and chile, with Marta bringing

him warm tortillas from the kitchen, Tony looked around sadly at this place that had been his home for the last six years. It was modest but comfortable, with several rooms sprawled haphazardly around a big tree-filled patio through which the morning sun now slanted brilliantly. One hammock swung in the shade of a full, glossy-leafed mango and another hung in the broad open-air corridor which ran the length of the house and served as both dining room and sitting room. Pancho Villa, the family parrot, chuckled to himself in an orange tree. A jet-black cat was industriously washing the faces of her six kittens in one corner of the veranda.

It was home—and the thought of leaving it made the tortillas stick in Tony's throat.

He knew the city. He had visited there on two occasions with his uncle and the memory made him shudder. It was like another country to him—a foreign land. Beautiful, yes, with its wide boulevards, skyscrapers, glittering shops and fine schools. But it was a place completely alien to the coast people.

There, on the great plateau more than seven thousand feet high, the air was dry and thin. The nights were cold and even the days were usually chilly. One had to dress in stiff woolen clothes and heavy shoes. The bustle and roar of the traffic was appalling. But worst of all, there was a cool formality about the people that froze Tony's heart, accustomed as he was to the easygoing, friendly casualness of the Acapulqueños.

Uncle Juan doubtless belonged in that atmosphere. And Tony had no quarrel with the preferences of other people. He only knew, with absolute certainty, that he himself would die in those surroundings. Literally die. Waste and wither as the tropical plants did when they were transported to a colder climate.

Suddenly he got up from the table with an abrupt movement that toppled his chair back.

"I've had enough," he called to Marta in the kitchen. "Don't heat more tortillas for me. I'll see you later."

And before she could answer, he was gone. He just had to get away by himself to think, to make plans, to consider this terrible, impossible ultimatum that Uncle Juan had forced on him!

He was halfway to the docks when he suddenly remembered his diving date with Peter. After a moment's hesitation, he went back to the house for his diving mask and rubber kick fins. The expedition underwater would help to clear his mind, he thought. And a chance to use an aqualung was not to be spurned—not by Tony—even during a crisis like this.

Like all Acapulco boys, he had known how to skin dive with a mask, almost from the time he had learned to walk and swim. It was not until three years ago that he had learned to dive with an aqualung, when one of the wealthier boys in the neighborhood had owned the equipment and generously loaned it often. However, the boy had since moved away and Tony's only opportunity to use an aqualung had been occasional times when the professional divers gave him odd jobs which they didn't want themselves.

Although it was not yet ten o'clock, Peter was already at the appointed spot on the beach when he arrived. He was sitting with his arms folded around his bony knees, watching the bathers and water skiers with a thoughtful expression in his blue eyes. Beside him, on the sand, was a pile of heavy equipment: two tanks of compressed air, lead belts, masks and fins.

"How did you ever get all that stuff down here by yourself—and where did you get it?" Tony asked curiously.

Peter smiled. "Dad helped me carry it down from the skin diving shop on the coast boulevard," he said. "He rented it. You see, this is my birthday. I told him this was what I wanted for a present—to rent this stuff for us."

"*Vaya!*" Tony pulled his mind away from his own problems. "*Felicidades, amigo!*" He put his arm around Peter's shoulders and pounded his back in the customary Mexican birthday embrace. "Why didn't you tell me this morning? I would have sung you the *mañanitas!* You know what the *mañanitas* are?"

"Sure," Peter answered shyly. "The birthday serenades. I've heard them many times since we came to Mexico. It's a nice custom."

"How old are you today?" Tony asked.

"Fifteen."

"Not much younger than me," Tony mused. "Somehow you seem younger than that, even."

"I've always been kind of small for my age," Peter said and then hurried on, as though wanting to leave that subject. "Where do we go for this skin diving, Tony?"

"Roqueta Island is best, around the rocks. I'll get one of my launchman friends to take us over."

When they had unloaded their gear on the rocky end

of Roqueta Beach, half an hour later, Tony stood looking down at it, a strange little smile on his face.

"You've never been underwater with an aqualung at all?" he asked thoughtfully.

"No. I've wanted to go ever since we came to Acapulco but—well, it costs quite a bit. You know this matter of money."

"Yes," Tony said heavily, his own problem bearing down on him again. "How well I know this matter of money!"

"I've looked below the surface with just a mask," Peter added in an eager voice. "It's wonderful under there! I suppose going down with a tank of compressed air is about the same, only you don't have to hold your breath."

"No," Tony said carefully. "It's quite different." He hesitated. Not everyone felt as he did about diving. Better wait and see how Pedro reacted to it, before discussing it.

"Well," he said briskly. "Now there are a few important things to learn, and then we'll try you out."

Peter listened intently as Tony explained how to hold the rubber mouthpiece of the air hose, not too lightly, not too loosely; how to swallow his saliva if his ears began to hurt, or press the mask against his face, blowing through his nose, to equalize the pressure on the eardrums.

"Either way stops the pain in your ears," Tony said, "though we won't be going deep enough today for that to bother you much. Above all, don't get scared. Breathe naturally and lightly. The more deeply you breathe, the more air from the tanks you use up—and we want to make it last! One more thing: the rubber fins give your leg stroke so much power, you don't need to use your arms for swimming—just to guide you. And keep your kick slow and steady, like your breathing. That way you don't scare the fish."

He helped Peter put on the fins, the weighted belt, the rubber-rimmed glass diving mask. Then he slung the aqualung on his back, adjusting the harness and checking the loops of hose which ran from regulator to mouthpiece.

"It all feels pretty heavy now," Tony said, suppressing a smile as he saw Peter's knees buckle. "But once you're in the water, you'll see you have no weight at all. Walk out now till the water's up to your shoulders, stick your head under and practice breathing."

Tony quickly put on his own equipment and joined Peter in the clear blue, sun-dappled water. Before inserting his mouthpiece, he asked, "How's it going?"

Unable to talk, Peter made a circle of his thumb and forefinger to indicate that it was going fine.

"Okay, then we'll take a little cruise." Tony tried to keep the excitement out of his voice. "Stick close and if you need help, tap your tank with your fingernails. But I'll be watching you all the time. Take it easy and don't brush against the sea urchins on the rocks. Their spines break off under your skin and sometimes infect. And remember that underwater everything looks bigger than it is and closer to you."

Peter nodded and the two boys walked out over their heads, bubbles of expelled breath rising to the surface above them.

Peter was all right, Tony thought, watching him carefully at first. He breathed regularly and used the kick fins gently, propelling himself easily along the sandy bottom and obviously watching for shells, for he picked up a half-buried conch and waved it triumphantly in Tony's direction.

Tony nodded to show that he saw it. He was gliding along languidly at Peter's side and feeling, as he always did, the miracle and joy of being half fish in the dreamlike wonder of this other world which sometimes seemed to him the only place where he could be completely himself. Walled in silence, without weight or resistance, it was for him the land beyond the looking glass where everything, no matter how trancelike, finally made sense.

Moving through liquid blue silk, shot with gleams of sunlight, watching the dancing flicker of the brilliant tropical fish, he felt as though this were his own private domain—as though he alone had discovered it and knew all its siren songs. His problems always dropped away magically in this curious evening-blue world with its fantastic landscape of hills and plains and disheveled jewel-colored rocks. On the sandy bottom, red and purple sea fans moved as though in a breeze. Starfish and sea spiders crawled imperceptibly.

He glanced at Peter, wondering what his blond friend thought about it. Peter was paying no attention to him and Tony could tell nothing from his face, half covered by the mask.

Anyway, he certainly isn't afraid, Tony thought with satisfaction. There was usually at least one small scare during the first few minutes of skin-diving experience: a feeling of claustrophobia, an unwillingness to believe that the tanks of compressed air would really work. But Peter looked like a veteran already.

They drifted gradually deeper and suddenly Tony caught sight of a small octopus playing on a carpet of sand between the rocks. He made a mental note of the location.

"You stay right there, Señor Octopus," he told it silently. "Don't go wandering off! I'll be back for you before we go."

Peter was suspended, bemused, above a labyrinth of rocks and Tony propelled himself closer to look. A school of parrot fish was playing hide and seek in a rock castle. The boys watched for some time and then Tony touched Peter's bare shoulder and pointed back, toward the beach. Peter shook his head vehemently and Tony smiled inwardly but he pointed again, more insistently.

A few minutes later, in shallow water once more, Peter pushed back his mask and let the mouthpiece drop.

"Why did you want to come back so soon?" he asked angrily. "We were only out there a few minutes. We have an hour—"

Tony's smile was soft and pleased. "I can see you're going to make a real skin diver, Pedrito. We were under for *more* than an hour! The air lasted because we didn't go very deep."

"I don't believe it," Peter said flatly.

"Well, that tourist over there has a watch. Ask him."

"It seemed about five minutes." Peter's voice was incredulous.

"That's the way it is—when you're really caught up in it," Tony answered. "You like it, don't you, Pedro?"

For a moment Peter didn't answer. There was a musing, faraway look in his blue eyes. He was staring down at the shells in his hand but he wasn't really seeing them.

When he finally turned to Tony, his voice was strange, almost a hoarse whisper. "I tell you the truth, Tony, I never dreamed there was anything like this in the world! It's like dreams I've had of flying—floating. I—I don't know how to say it. It's like I was a different person—like I'd always be a different person from now on. It's—" He threw up his hands to indicate the futility of mere words.

"Welcome to the fraternity, brother," Tony said quietly. "You don't have to try to explain to me. *I know!* Once you've really felt it, it's one of the few things that seem to matter."

And maybe I have to leave it! he added to himself in sudden anguish, remembering again, and turning his face away so that Peter would not see his eyes.

"Wait for me," he said gruffly when he had control of himself. "I'm going out after that octopus I saw. It's small but it's something. There isn't time to look for lobster now."

Without waiting for Peter to answer, he put his mouthpiece in again and sank out of sight. He wasn't sure just how much air there was left in his tank. But remembering the conversation with Uncle Juan, somehow it didn't seem to matter. He meant to make the most of every second, from now on.

He had almost reached the spot where he had seen

the octopus when he was suddenly surrounded by clouds of small fish flying past him. And within seconds he knew the reason.

A six-foot hammerhead shark was cruising straight toward him!

Tony's instinct was to turn and swim for dear life. Instead he forced himself to freeze motionless, his heart thumping painfully.

3

Nothing Ventured,
Nothing Gained

TONY FOLLOWED THE SHARK WITH HIS EYES AS MUCH AS
he could while it circled around him, but he did not
move his body. Never had he seen a hammerhead so
close in to the swimming beaches before! But he had had
experience with sharks out deeper in the bay and he
knew that the best thing to do was to remain perfectly
quiet and, above all, not to surface.

Motion—and particularly the motion of dangling feet
—might tempt the shark to pursue and sample a mouthful of leg. But it took a lot of will power not to move!
Under the diving mask, Tony could feel perspiration
stinging his eyes as the ugly creature circled once—twice
—three times—slowly coming nearer. The hammerhead
was obviously very curious about this strange, goggled,
two-legged fish that kept expelling bubbles into the
water.

The shark was now less than four feet from him,
swimming at an angle in order to peer from the eyes

grotesquely placed at either end of the flat, hammer-shaped head. Tony was wondering how much longer he could stand the motionless suspense when suddenly, with the barest flick of its forked tail, the creature turned and sailed disdainfully away into the deeper blue water.

Tony drew a long deep breath of the air in his tank and shook his head in groggy relief. The sharks in Acapulco waters were not man-eaters and were generally considered harmless, unless there was blood in the water. Nevertheless, even the most fearless skin divers agreed that sharks—any sharks—were unpredictable, and Tony could not remember when he had spent a more acutely uncomfortable three minutes!

He turned to go back to the beach and then suddenly remembered what he had come for. The little octopus had taken refuge from the shark but Tony could see it now, emerging cautiously from the rocks where it had hidden.

Might as well get it, since I'm here, he thought.

Grasping his short spear, he went on down to the bottom. But just as he impaled the octopus, with one swift thrust, he felt as though he were choking and realized that air was no longer coming through his mouthpiece. Flicking on the safety valve at the bottom of the air tank, he drove the spear deeper and turned it upright, in order not to lose the imprisoned wriggler. Then he kicked toward shore, breathing as lightly as possible.

His knees were a bit rubbery as he waded through the shallow water to the beach where Peter was waiting, looking rather disgruntled.

"You were gone a long time," he said reproachfully. "So you see there *was* a lot of air left in your tank—and in mine, too, probably."

Tony shook his head. "I turned on the reserve supply and even at that, I just made it back," he said, panting. He was glad to have a good excuse for his breathlessness. He didn't intend to spoil Peter's first skin-diving experience with tales of sharks! Another time—if there was another time—he would caution him in a casual way.

Peter was distracted from his reproaches by the octopus, which was straining madly to get off the gaff.

"Why don't you kill it and put it out of its misery?" he asked.

"If we're going to eat it, we want it to stay alive as long as possible," Tony answered reasonably. "Don't worry, Pedro. As soon as we get a boat, I'll take the spear out and you'll see it'll be as lively as ever. An octopus has nine lives, like a cat!"

They didn't have to wait long for a ride. Chico, a boy Tony had known from childhood, agreed cheerfully to take them back to the mainland in the boat on which he worked.

Tony was quiet as the launch chugged away from the island. He had forgotten the shark now and was thinking again about the all-important problem of staying in Acapulco.

It was strange, he mused, how you took things for granted until the threat of losing them sharpened your awareness, and then it all seemed new and you longed for the lost moments when you hadn't really looked and felt and smelled and touched, with every part of your senses.

Had the bay ever been quite this beautiful before? Now, at noon, it was such a dancing, dazzling blue that it hurt the eyes to look at it. He stared through the mouth of the bay to the open Pacific beyond—that flat, infinitely mysterious expanse that went on and on to the very edge of the world. He looked behind him at the emerald island they had just left, its slopes rising steep up from the water to the lighthouse on the peak. He breathed deeply of the faintly salty, faintly fishy air. He gazed ahead at Caleta Beach, its smooth curve of white sand sprinkled with bathers and fringed in the background with coconut palms that waved gently in the breeze.

He couldn't give it all up! He *wouldn't* give it up without a mighty struggle!

"That's quite a haul you have there, Tony—that enormous octopus." Chico's teasing voice broke into his thoughts. "I'd be ashamed to take a baby like that away from its mother!"

"If I'd seen the mother, I'd have taken her and left the baby." Tony grinned, trying to put his problems out of his mind.

"They are a strange fish, aren't they?" Peter said wonderingly. He had hardly taken his eyes from it since Tony released it in the launch where it now crawled back and forth, rage and fear making it swell and change color from brilliant yellow to mottled brown and then to yellow again, as it desperately looked for a way back to its home in the blue depths.

Poor octopus! Tony thought. Aloud he said, "Those suction cups on its tentacles are amazingly strong. Even on a young one like this. Pick it up, Pedro, and you'll see."

"No thanks." Peter made a face. "I'll take your word for it."

Chico laughed.

"Pedro feels sorry for it," Tony said. "Tell you the truth, so do I. I hate to take them, especially the little ones. But Aunt Raquel likes octopus and it will be something, at least, to carry home. There wasn't time to look for a lobster farther out in the rocks."

"You probably wouldn't have found your lobster, anyway," Chico said. "The truth is, this bay is pretty well fished out—of things like shell fish, I mean—between the commercial skin divers who are doing it for money, and the tourists who are doing it for fun."

"I'm afraid you're right," Tony said, depressed again. It was what he himself had been thinking during the skin-diving trip. And it wasn't going to help him make the necessary money during these crucial next three months!

"If a person had a good-sized boat to go up and down the coast," he brooded aloud. "There is everything within a day's run of here—wonderful lobster caves, big oyster beds, all kinds of sea food—"

"There's not so much close by, any more," Chico objected. "And if you go any distance, you have to have some kind of refrigeration. No, I'll tell you, the only way to make money in Acapulco now is working with the tourists. You know lots of English, Tony. Maybe we could go into business together, eh? Get rich quick like some of these other people!"

"What kind of business?" Tony asked cautiously.

"Almost any kind, *hombre!* Guiding tourists. Taking them for rides—in more ways than one!" He glanced at Peter out of the corner of his eye.

"You needn't look at him. He's not a tourist." Tony put his hand on Peter's shoulder. "He's an Acapulqueño now. *Verdad,* Pedro?"

Peter nodded, grinning.

"A little capital is all one needs," Chico went on confidently. "They spend money for *anything*—the gringos and the rich Mexicans from Mexico City, too."

"And the capital?" Tony asked ironically. "You provide it?"

"Your uncle has money." Chico's eyes were crafty.

Tony grunted. "You don't know my uncle! In the first place, he really doesn't have a lot of money. And in the second place, he wouldn't invest a cent in any business that has anything to do with the sea."

"Well, maybe we could do it without capital." Chico shrugged as he guided the launch onto the beach. "Come around, anyway, and we'll talk it over."

"Okay. And thanks for the ride."

Tony draped the octopus over his arm like a scarf and he and Peter jumped out, loading themselves down with the skin-diving gear.

Chico, too, Tony thought as they walked down the beach to where they could cut over to the skin-diving shop on the coast boulevard. Everyone was trying to figure out ways of getting some of the tourist money!

He could remember when he and Chico used to spend whole days out around the edges of the bay, diving for fun and then lying in the sun on the polished rock shelves, listening to the low, insistent speaking of the water as it licked around them. That was toward the end of those golden years when Tony's father was still alive—when no one worried much about money or about anything except food. And food could be picked from the sea with one's bare hands.

Chico had been different then. But everyone and everything had been different then. There were tourists then, too, but they hadn't quite taken over the entire town. The days had been all-bright, unworried, sun-spangled dreams. How long ago it seemed! Another lifetime!

Tony sighed. He felt as though he were sixty, instead of not quite sixteen.

"You act as though you'd lost your last friend. Didn't you like the skin diving?"

Peter's voice was faintly accusing and Tony, returning to the present, remembered that the blond boy had generously shared his birthday gift, the aqualung trip. He knew that it wasn't the money invested that made Peter reproachful; it was something else. The underwater excursion had been a revelation to Peter and he couldn't understand why anyone should be downcast after such an experience.

Tony suddenly decided to tell his friend about the interview with Uncle Juan.

"Forgive me, Pedro," he said quietly. "I liked the diving, all right. I always like it! But I have a problem. Wait till we drop this heavy stuff and then I'll tell you about it."

They left the octopus in a small aquarium at the skin-diving shop, to be collected later, and went up on the hill near the Caleta Hotel in the shade. They sat for several minutes without speaking. That was another nice thing about Pedro, Tony thought. He didn't have to talk all the time, like some gringos. He had a kind of Mexican patience.

"It's my uncle," Tony said finally, in a heavy voice. "He's moving the family back to Mexico City, the end of January. And he wants me to go with them."

"To *stay?*"

The horror in Peter's voice was oddly comforting to Tony. Here was someone who felt as he did about the sea and about Acapulco. Pedro—although he was a North American and had never seen this coast town until three months ago—understood better than anyone else that for Tony, leaving Acapulco was the end of the world.

Tony nodded unhappily.

"He wants me to work in a little hotel he has in the capital, learning the business. And go at night to a hotel school they have in the city. He wants me to be a hotel man." Tony's voice sounded strange, even to his own ears, and he coughed to dislodge whatever it was that was stuck in his throat.

"I—I never heard of anything so crazy!" Peter sputtered, staring at Tony's strong, smooth-muscled brown shoulders, his earnest, unhappy black eyes. To the American boy, Tony seemed as much a part of this tropical paradise as the turquoise water, the resilient palms, and the drying fish nets. It was impossible to even imagine him in any other setting. "You—a hotel man in the city. It's insane! I—I'd run away, first."

Tony put a hand gratefully on his friend's thin shoulder but he didn't look at him. He was looking across the bay to the open sea.

"That's what I'd like to do," he admitted, after a moment. "But there's something you don't know about this, Pedro. My father died when I was nine and my sister Marta was eight. Uncle Juan came down from the city, then, with the idea of taking us back there to live. But he had some heart trouble—the doctor had already told him he ought to live at sea level instead of at that high altitude of the capital—so he and Aunt Raquel decided to lease their hotel in Mexico City and move here for a while. I thought *of course* that once they got used to Acapulco, they'd want to stay for good."

Tony's voice trailed off thinly, but then he went on. "They took Marta and me in as if we were their own children and gave us a home and schooling. They weren't rich, either, and they have two girls of their own, a little younger than Marta. For myself, I wouldn't have cared if they adopted us or not. But Marta—well, she is my sister and I am fond of her. She wants to be a teacher. I feel obliged to Uncle Juan for taking care of her—of us. And another thing, I am the only boy. I think Uncle Juan always wanted a son, to carry on his business."

"I see," Peter said slowly. "That makes it a little different, I guess, but even so, I should think your uncle could see that the city is no place for you. Surely—"

"He knows a different side of me than you do," Tony

explained hopelessly. "You see, all this time while I studied in school and helped him in the store, I was thinking that if I worked hard enough I'd get what I wanted in the end." He sighed. "I fixed things for myself! I've convinced him that I'd make a good hotel man because I speak English to his American customers in the store and try to please them.

"So now," he finished bitterly, "I go to the capital and carry the expensive bags of rich people and bring them ice and say, 'Yes, sir' and 'No, sir' and 'Thank you, sir' and learn to bow and scrape and judge people by the amount they pay in tips."

"You'd never judge people that way," Peter said positively.

Tony went on as though he were talking to himself. "If my uncle was at all like my father was," he muttered, "but he couldn't be more different! Uncle Juan doesn't like the sea. I think he's afraid of it. He's never understood the coast people. Aunt Raquel—she's more like an Acapulqueña, comfortable and easygoing. Uncle Juan likes everything just so, very stiff and formal."

"But none of that matters. You can't go," Peter repeated stubbornly. "You'd be as out of place in the city as your uncle is here."

"Unless I can save two thousand pesos toward a boat by the end of January," Tony said grimly, "I have to go. That's what he said and he never changes his mind."

Peter was silent. Two thousand pesos was only one hundred and sixty dollars in American money but to Peter, as to Tony, it seemed nothing less than a fortune.

"That's a lot of money," he agreed gloomily, after a moment. "I wish I could help. I wish my father had the money to buy a boat and you and I could use it together and have a business. But you know how it is with us. We came here because Dad thought the outdoor life would be good for me and because we could live more cheaply in Mexico while he was writing his book. We've only got the little he saved when he was a newspaperman."

Tony nodded. "I couldn't take anything from you, anyway. The whole point is that Uncle Juan wants me to earn it myself. And there's another angle to it: on account of what he said about my father, now I've got to prove to him that people who live from fishing and skin diving aren't necessarily bums! My father was a wonderful man, Pedro, even if he didn't make much money."

"I've never heard you mention your mother," Peter ventured.

"She died when my sister was born," Tony explained, "so my father had the whole care of us, you see. He loved Marta and me a lot and he made us happy. That's more important than money, I think. Maybe you have to really love *money* to be good at earning it. It just never seemed one of the important things to my father—and it doesn't to me, either."

"It's necessary though, sometimes," Peter sighed, knowing from experience what it was like to be without it. "Well, maybe you can do it, Tony! What about that Chico and his plans?"

Tony shook his head doubtfully. "I don't think Chico is up to any good, Pedrito. I'll talk to him. But he's changed. A lot of the boys I used to know have changed. It's the tourist business that's done it. Maybe that's why Uncle Juan talks about beach bums."

"*Tony!*" The word exploded from Peter, and his blue eyes were suddenly blazing with excitement. "I just thought of something! While I was waiting for you on the beach this morning, one of the glass-bottomed boats came back, and they carried off a diver. I heard the boys say that he'd slipped and broken his ankle when he climbed up to dive from some high rocks—putting on an extra show for the tourists. Maybe you could get his job!"

"Kowtowing to tourists," Tony said distastefully, but his face gradually brightened. "At least it would be a beginning—and doing something I like—skin diving! They don't pay those boys much, but there are tips and commissions." He grinned suddenly. "You know that expression in Spanish: '*Solo el que no monta, no cae*'?"

"'Only he who does not mount, does not fall,'" Peter translated thoughtfully. "I like the English one better: 'Nothing ventured, nothing gained!'"

"Nothing ventured, nothing gained." Tony tried it on his tongue and nodded. "Yes, I like that better, too! Come on, Pedro, let's see if that job's taken! What was the name of the launch?"

"*Pelicano*, I think. Yes, I'm sure that was it."

"That's Captain García's boat. I've heard he's pretty good to work for. Keep your fingers crossed, Pedrito!"

4

Double Celebration

"I just hired a boy ten minutes ago," Captain García said. "Sorry, son."

Tony's heart sank to his bare toes. Probably there were other jobs to be had in Acapulco but it seemed like a bad omen, not getting this first one. He stared at the captain helplessly, wanting to ask if the other boy was as good a skin diver as he, Tony, was, and if he could speak as much English. But of course he couldn't say it just like that.

"He's older than you are," the captain remarked, as though answering the silent questions. "And he's had a little more experience."

"I'm old for my age," Tony muttered, feeling at the moment that it was certainly the truth.

"You might keep in touch with me," Captain García said, pulling out a desk drawer in a signal of dismissal. "There might be something else, later."

Tony couldn't think of any reason for staying. "Well, thanks, anyway," he murmured disconsolately, moving toward the door. "*Adiós.*"

He was so wrapped up in his disappointment that he didn't see the tall American tourist outside until he had run right into him.

"*Dispénseme,*" he said automatically. Then, realizing to whom he spoke, he repeated it in English, "Excuse me, sir."

"That's all right." The man smiled. "Maybe you can tell me where to find a Captain García? And do you know if he speaks English?"

"His office is here," Tony answered. Glancing at the door, which he had left ajar, an idea struck him and he went on, raising his voice slightly, "But he doesn't speak much English. Can I help you? I'll translate if you want to talk to him."

"That would be nice of you," the tourist said, looking at him more closely. "I want to ask about chartering one of his boats to take out a private party of people."

"Just a minute." Tony knocked on the captain's door again and stuck his head in. "Excuse me, Captain, but there is a North American here, wanting to make an arrangement with you."

Captain García looked a little harassed. "*Caramba,* my partner, who speaks English, is at dinner. Ask him to come back later, boy."

"He would probably go to another boat owner," Tony said. "I have told him I would translate, if you like."

The captain glanced at Tony with shrewd eyes and a faint smile touched the corners of his mouth.

"All right." He shrugged his shoulders. "Ask him to come in."

Tony ushered the tourist into the office, pulled out a

chair for him and then stood between them, translating the exchange in a businesslike way.

The American was a member of a lawyers' convention which was ending up a Mexican trip with a few days' vacation in Acapulco. They wanted to take a boat for an entire day, sight-seeing along the coast.

When the financial arrangements were settled to the satisfaction of both parties, the tourist said to Tony, "Will you be one of the crew? Tell the captain we would like to have you. You've been very obliging and courteous and you speak better English than most of the boat boys we've had occasion to deal with."

Tony translated this word for word, his face expressionless, his gaze fixed out of the window.

There was a brief silence and finally Tony glanced at the captain to find the man looking at him suspiciously.

"This is a rather strange coincidence, isn't it? You're certain it was not prearranged?"

"Captain!" Tony's voice was pained. "I never saw this man in my life until I bumped into him outside your door just now. I can prove it."

He was going to go on and admit that it had seemed an opportunity to show how much English he knew, but the captain interrupted him: "All right." His voice was dry. "I'll take your word for it. You may tell the señor that you are not on the crew of the larger boat but if he wishes the pleasure of your company, he can take a glass-bottomed boat trip on the *Pelicano*."

Tony looked at him with shining eyes. "You mean—"

"Yes, you're hired," Captain García said shortly. "I'll give that other boy something else to do. He does not have quite as much English as you do—nor your way with people, I think."

"What does he say?" asked the tourist, curiously.

Tony explained briefly that he was a skin diver and regretted that he could not accompany the chartered boat. The business was concluded and five minutes later, he rejoined Peter on the beach.

"I got it!" he yelled triumphantly. "Fifteen pesos a day to start—and if I'm good, he says he'll raise it later. But I got it by the purest accident!"

He went on to tell about the coincidence of the tourist and how he had convinced the captain of his proficiency in English. Peter listened with a little smile on his face, and suddenly Tony broke off.

"What are you grinning about?" he demanded.

"Nothing." Peter's face was innocent.

"You sent that tourist up there!" Tony could see by Peter's expression that he had guessed right. "The captain said he thought it was a put-up job and I told him it wasn't!"

"Well, it wasn't," Peter said, smiling broadly now. "If a man on the beach asks me where he can charter a boat and I send him to the only captain I know about, that's hardly a put-up job, is it? But wasn't it lucky he came along just then, Tony!"

They looked at each other and burst out laughing. Tony clapped the blond boy on the back.

"You are a real friend, Pedro! Getting that job meant a lot to me. At least it will prove to Uncle Juan that I mean business!"

And it may lead to something else more profitable, he added to himself. Anyway, it was a lot better to be doing something—going somewhere—than just standing still and worrying. Sometimes, if you just kept on going, the way opened up. . . .

"I'm starved!" he said abruptly as they walked back down the beach. "Come on, we'll have lunch at Caletilla. My treat, this time! I have a friend who manages one of the restaurants and I can get credit."

"You shouldn't begin to spend your money already," Peter said seriously. "You're going to save it for a boat, remember?"

"You sound like Uncle Juan." Tony grinned. "Just this once, we celebrate. It won't cost much. And I owe you something for the skin diving trip and for the job."

"You don't owe me anything!"

But Peter was hungry, too, and he allowed himself to be led to one of the outdoor tables under the trees on Caletilla, twin beach to Caleta.

"*Hola*, Julio!" Tony called.

A pleasantly homely boy came out to the table from the restaurant inside.

"Tony! What a surprise! I never see you any more!"

Tony clapped him on the shoulder. "I've been around, brother. Mostly working in that store of my uncle's. Julio, this is Pedro—Peter Carson, in English. He is also my brother—my blond brother! He is nine-tenths Acapulqueño now. You should see the way he took to skin diving this morning!"

Julio and Peter shook hands, grinning.

"Julio finished school two years ago—lucky man," Tony told Peter. "He's worked up fast to managing this restaurant. He'll probably own it soon."

"That's doubtful," Julio laughed.

Peter thought of something. "What are you going to do about school now, Tony? You'll have to work in the mornings."

"I won't go." Tony shrugged. "I can make it up later. With only three months to earn this money, I can't use any of the time on school. Uncle Juan will understand that."

Julio lifted an inquiring eyebrow.

"You'll see me around a lot more, from now on," Tony told him. "Pedro, here, got me a job on a glass-bottomed boat!"

"He got it himself." Peter smiled at Julio.

"Well, that'll be fine—having you around the beach all the time," Julio said. "You can come over here and eat oysters between trips."

"A lot of money I'd save that way!" Tony laughed. "If I eat oysters, I'll dive for them myself. I have to make money—lots of money—in the next three months, Julio. I'll tell you about it later. At the moment, we are dying of hunger. What do you suggest that will fill the hole in our middles—cheap?"

"You wait. I'll fix you up!"

Julio hurried away, and Tony and Peter smiled at each other.

"He's a fine boy—Julio," Tony said. "He's only eighteen but he's steady, and he has a lot of sense. If you ever need help on the beach, come to him."

They leaned back, feeling like millionaires. The sun, slanting into afternoon, dappled the outdoor tables with patterns of light and shadows. Bathers with water dripping from their wet suits sat around leisurely drinking *refrescos* and eating sea food. Everyone seemed comfortable and contented with the sparkling day, the cool breeze and the shimmering blue bay. A woman put twenty centavos in the juke machine and the silky air pulsed with the strains of "Acapulqueña Linda," a half-sad, half-gay song about the beauty of Acapulco and of an Acapulco girl.

"What a beautiful song!" Peter said. "You know, Tony, this really is the most wonderful place in the world." His voice was almost hushed. "And you know something else? I suppose this will sound crazy to you—but I feel as though I had been born here. As though I'd never lived anywhere else. I feel as though it's *mine*, some way."

Tony nodded. "It doesn't sound crazy to me. I think people often get born in the wrong places. Where *were* you born, Pedro?"

"Indianapolis, Indiana."

"What a mouthful!" Tony laughed.

Peter smiled. "No more of a mouthful than Chilpancingo, Guerrero!" he retorted, naming a city to the north of Acapulco. "It all depends on which mouthful you're used to!"

"I guess so," Tony agreed. "What is it like—Indianapolis?" he added curiously.

"Well, I don't really know much about it," Peter answered. "I was born there but we moved to Detroit,

Michigan, when I was five, and then to Chicago, Illinois, after my mother died, and then—"

"*Caramba!*" Tony looked at his blond friend with astonishment. "Why did you move around so much? Were the police after your father?"

Peter laughed. "Not that I know of," he said, still grinning, "but I'll ask him when I get home! Seriously, I guess he was always looking for something, Tony— maybe a job he liked better. He's always been in some kind of newspaper work but he never really liked it. He isn't the type. He should have been a college professor, or in research. Newspapermen live under pressure and Dad finally got stomach ulcers from it. He's been happier in Mexico, writing this book, than he's been ever since my mother died."

"What kind of a book is he writing?"

"A historical novel—a real long one. I don't know if he'll ever sell it, or if he'll ever finish it, but it doesn't matter much, as long as he's happy."

Peter's voice was gently affectionate, as though he were talking about a child, and Tony looked at him curiously. At times, he thought, Pedro seemed very young, younger than fifteen, but at other times he sounded like an old man.

"Wasn't it hard on you—moving around so much?" Tony asked, getting the conversation back on his own level. "How would you know who you really *were*, in all those new places? And how would you ever have any friends?" He couldn't imagine such a life, himself.

"I didn't think much about it," Peter said. "People in

the United States do move around a l
they're more restless than Mexicans, in
Chicago wasn't so very different from Detr
from Indianapolis, except in size. The schools w
the same, and the kids were about the same,
didn't take very long to make new friends."

"Detroit is where they make all the cars, isn't it?"

"Not all of them. But it does have a lot of automobile factories."

"Well, tell me about it," Tony said. "Does it look like Mexico City?"

"Like some parts of Mexico City, I guess—some of the residential parts and the shopping districts," Peter said slowly. "But Detroit and Chicago are a lot different from Mexico in most ways. There aren't any mountains around them, for example, but there are a lot of big lakes. And there aren't any real old buildings like some of those in Mexico City. You don't get the feeling of a long history, like you do in Mexico."

"The history of the United States is short, compared to ours," Tony nodded. He knew that much from school.

But he wasn't interested in history. He wanted concrete facts about Peter's life in the States and he had his mouth open to ask another question when he saw that Julio had returned, bringing two plates with small pieces of meat swimming in rich, savory-smelling brown sauce. He also brought a small bowl of chopped avocados and tomatoes, a larger bowl of black beans and a stack of tortillas wrapped in a white napkin.

"*Ayee!* A feast!" Tony looked at Julio, his black eyes gleaming. "This is no cheap meal, *amigo!*"

21100

This time you are my guests. Next time I charge you double!"

"You see what I mean?" Tony said to Peter. "Always cultivate friends who are in the restaurant business! This was going to be my birthday present to you. Now it's Julio's, instead."

"Today is your *cumpleaños?*" Julio asked Peter, surprised.

The blond boy nodded shyly.

"You should have told me, Tony," Julio reproached. "I'd have made it a little more festive."

"It's perfect," Peter assured him, beginning to eat hungrily.

"Well, at least we can have the *mañanitas!*" Julio let out a piercing whistle to call the trio of musicians who strolled among the tables, offering their songs to tourists.

"Oh, please—no," Peter protested, turning red.

"But why not? You can't have a birthday dinner, however poor, without *mañanitas.* Especially since they cost nothing! The *músicos* are my friends."

He turned to the approaching trio. "*Las mañanitas, amigos!* For the blond Acapulqueño!"

Immediately the musicians launched into the best known and most loved tune of Mexico, and at once all the Mexicans within earshot looked around, smiling, to see whose birthday it was. Many of them even joined in the chorus and Peter sat, his face fiery with embarrassment, while the people at their end of the bench serenaded him and then heartily applauded him at the end, as was the custom.

Peter half rose to his feet and ducked his head in bashful acknowledgment; then sat down, relieved, as the musicians drifted away and attention was no longer focused on their table.

"Okay, now you can eat." Julio grinned at him. "And if it is cold, tell me and I'll warm it up."

"I guess I never had so much fuss made over my birthday," Peter murmured.

"Never?" Tony looked at him wonderingly. "Not in Indianapolis or Detroit or Chicago? Well, you'll get used to it, Pedro, if you stay in Mexico. Birthdays are big days here."

"This was nothing," Julio added. "The best we could do on short notice." He straddled a chair. "Now tell me about your job, Tony. What boat are you going to be working on?"

"The *Pelicano*." Tony's voice was muffled by a mouthful of tortilla. "Captain García. He seems a decent sort."

Julio frowned but the other two boys were too busy eating to notice.

"How did you happen to get the job? There have been two boys working that boat."

Peter explained about the accident.

"Was it a short boy with curly hair who was hurt, or the tall one?" Julio's voice was tense and Tony looked at him.

"He was a short boy," Peter answered.

Tony stopped eating. "What's the matter, Julio?"

"Nothing." Julio jumped up. "Excuse me a moment. I go to see about things in the kitchen. Eat well, *muchachos*."

They were finishing the last of the tortillas and the beans when Julio came back.

"Was it all right?" he asked. "Did it fill the cavity?"

"A meal for kings," Tony answered gratefully. "I am full up to here." He put his hand just under his chin. "*Muchas gracias, amigo*. And now tell me why you are so gloomy about the *Pelicano*. I could tell from your face there's something wrong."

"It's nothing, really." Julio's voice was reluctant. "It's only that the tall boy you'll have to work with, Tony, is Lencho Ramirez."

Tony drew in his breath. "Yes, of course I've heard of him," he said. "He has a bad reputation, hasn't he?"

Julio nodded. "He's a troublemaker. Just don't let him get under your skin, that's the main thing."

"I'll handle him," Tony boasted, with more assurance than he felt. He had heard a good deal about Lencho. "Well, we must be getting back now, eh, Pedro?"

"Yes. Many thanks for the birthday party," Peter said to Julio. "And I'm glad to know you."

"Equally, Pedro." Julio smiled at him and then turned seriously to Tony. "Promise me you'll be careful in your dealings with Lencho, Tony. He's a tough customer!"

5

The Glass–Bottomed Boat

Tony brought the launch up near the western end
of Roqueta Island, over rock caverns that lay about
twelve feet below the surface, and killed the motor.

"We're going to stop here," he announced in English
to the cargo of tourists who were leaning expectantly
over the glass-bottomed well of the boat. "Our diver
Lencho will go down and see what he can find for you.
Lencho is one of the best skin divers in Acapulco. He can
hold his breath under water for almost three minutes."

The words, although they were quite true, stuck in
his throat. They were part of an act—and Tony hated
acting. Lencho said the same thing about him when he,
Tony, was diving. People liked to feel that they were
being entertained by the best talent.

There were appropriate murmurs of appreciation from
the passengers, most of whom were middle-aged and
quite content to admire the exploits of youth from a
comfortable, spectator position.

Tony avoided looking at the one young passenger: a
trim, auburn-haired girl in white blouse and shorts who
sat in the middle of the boat. She made him uneasy. This

was her second ride on the *Pelicano*. On the first trip, yesterday, she had followed his every movement with something slightly more than the curious, impersonal interest of the average tourist, and it had embarrassed him. Also, he knew that it had annoyed Lencho, who considered himself irresistible to girls. Tony wanted to avoid trouble.

Lencho glanced at the girl now as he made his preparations in the bow of the boat, fitting rubber fins on his feet, molding the face mask over his eyes and nose, and picking up his spear. He stood for a moment, his bronze body clad only in black swim trunks, outlined against the turquoise sky. Then he sat down, swung his feet over the side of the boat and dropped into the water quietly, in order not to disturb whatever fish might be in the vicinity.

He's a born showman, Tony thought. Whether he's talking to them or whether he's diving, he's always showing off. He loves it—and they love it. And I hate it!

For five weeks now, he had been a partner to this performance several times a day and they had been the longest five weeks of his life. He loved to dive but he despised making a show of it. Even worse than that was the antagonism that had built up between Lencho and himself—a hatred so implacable and unremitting that Tony wondered if their passengers couldn't feel it simmering around them in the small boat!

A dozen times he had been on the point of quitting— and a dozen times he had looked apprehensively at the calendar, counted his slim savings and decided to try it a while longer. Even though each day seemed endless, time was slipping away from him much too fast. November business had not been as good as usual. There had been days when the *Pelicano* had not gone out at all. Now it was almost the middle of December and he had saved less than four hundred pesos. There were only seven short weeks to accumulate the balance of the two thousand that Uncle Juan had set as the minimum toward a first payment on a fishing boat. And if he didn't make it—

He rubbed his forehead with the back of his hand as though to rub away the impossible alternative, and he suddenly realized that some of the passengers were looking at him curiously. He dragged his mind from his problems to the present business.

"Now watch through the glass bottom," he said briskly, mechanically repeating the spiel that Lencho had taught him five weeks ago. "Our boy will be coming under the boat to say hello to you before he goes down to say hello to the fish."

His audience of eleven smiled dutifully, their eyes glued again on the glass as Lencho swam under the launch, grinning and waving his spear. Then he finned on down toward the rock caverns. A few brilliantly colored fish moved lazily out of his path.

"How exotic looking those yellow and black things are!" exclaimed one of the American women.

"Those are mariposas, madam—butterfly fish."

"They don't seem to pay any attention at all to the diver!"

"We have them trained," Tony said, using one of Lencho's thin jokes. "They think we're just a new and unusually ugly kind of big fish."

His eyes flickered toward the auburn-haired girl as he wondered uncomfortably if she had heard this same thing from Lencho yesterday when he, Tony, was diving. There was a little smile on her lips but her gray eyes remained fixed on the glass below.

Lencho was out of sight behind a huge boulder. There was nothing to see but the mariposas and a few parrot fish, moving languidly among the rocks carpeted with seaweed. A small sea bass hurried by, as though on some important errand.

Tony tried to think of something to tell his passengers during the wait. There were a great many things that he knew about the sea which might interest them. Since people always seemed to be fascinated by sea monsters, he could tell them of his own encounter with a moray eel, a couple of years ago. He had angled into an underwater cave, trying to hook a lobster, and had come within half an inch of having his hand snapped off by the razor teeth of a large brownish-green moray. After that episode, he had decided not to poke around in rock crevasses barehanded! Or he could tell them about the hammerhead shark he had seen while diving with Pedro, a few weeks ago. Or the needlefish which were not intentionally aggressive but were an accidental hazard to the night fishermen; skimming the surface with amazing speed, they sometimes leaped so far out of water that their long, sharp snouts were capable of stabbing straight into the chests of the unwary. Or the awe-inspiring sight of a giant manta ray, its eighteen-foot wingspread outlined by the phosphorescence in the water, rising near a tiny *canoa* in the darkness of the ocean at night, the enormous fins moving slowly like the wings of a mammoth bird of the sea. Although the manta rays had no teeth and ate only plankton, they had their element of danger, too, since one of their nocturnal sports was to leap out of the sea and come down on it again with the resounding crash of a ton of flesh on water—the waves from which could easily swamp the small craft of the night fishermen.

These and many other things he would gladly have shared with the curious tourists. But, for one thing, he didn't want to scare them away from the beaches. Actually, there were comparatively few hazards to swimmers in Acapulco waters. Moray eels were a rarity and never attacked unless you invaded their homes in the rocks. Sharks never seemed to molest the bathers; and unless the tourists went night fishing in a *canoa*, which was unlikely, they'd never see a leaping needlefish or a manta ray. But the main reason he didn't tell them was because he usually found himself tongue-tied when confronted by an audience—and even more so today, with the gray eyes of the red-haired girl glancing in his direction from time to time, as though she sensed his embarrassment and was amused by it.

He just wasn't good at this talking business, and he knew it. Most of the time since he had worked on the *Pelicano,* he had done the diving while Lencho talked, and he liked it much better that way. A week ago, however, Lencho had announced abruptly that they would take turns, as most of the other boys on the glass-bottomed boats did.

"I don't see how he can hold his breath that long!" breathed an elderly man with gray hair. "Seems as though he's been under at least ten minutes!"

Tony had made a bet with himself that someone would say that, every trip. So far he had won all the bets.

"It always seems longer than it actually is," he said gently. "Here he comes now."

Lencho appeared through the glass, holding a sea urchin in one hand and a sea cucumber in the other. Pretty poor pickings to start with, Tony thought, from a whole ocean. Lencho surfaced beside the boat, handed the trophies to Tony, looked at the auburn-haired girl, pumped his lungs with air and went down again.

"This is the short-spined, purple sea urchin—one of several different varieties we have around Acapulco," Tony recited. "You must be careful not to step on them when you are swimming around rocks because their spines are difficult to get out, once they enter your skin, and they're likely to cause an infection."

"And yet you handle it!" cried one of the lady tourists. They always said that, too.

"We know how," Tony told her modestly.

"Always make the tourist think you know everything and can do things he can't do," Lencho had counseled. "That's one way to get their interest."

"The insides of these urchins are considered a delicacy like caviar in some parts of the world," Tony continued his recital, "but here we use it chiefly for bait. I will show you how the fish love it."

He cut out the inside of the squirming, spiny mass, dropped it into the water close to the boat and instantly, through the glass bottom, they could see a shimmering cloud of small silvery fish, fighting for a nibble.

The tourists hung over the glass, entranced. Only the girl was sitting upright, her eyes on Tony. So far, on the trip, she had not said a single word. She made him distinctly uncomfortable.

"This must be very dull for you, Señorita," he said abruptly. "You have seen and heard it all before—perhaps many times before."

"I never get tired of it," she answered quietly. "I find everything about the sea interesting. The fish, the boats —and the people who work on the water."

Tony felt his ears reddening. "Now the sea cucumber—" he began hurriedly, picking up the small, flabby, animal-like fish.

On and on, forever and ever, he thought, as the lecture continued. He was aware that his voice sounded dry from repetition and distaste. He talked for only twenty minutes, as Lencho periodically delivered souvenirs, but it seemed to him that he had been explaining elementary sea lore for at least an hour, by the time the other boy climbed back into the boat and was greeted with a spatter of applause.

The red-haired girl did not applaud but she gave Lencho a little smile which he acknowledged with a rather insolent grin.

The other passengers were absorbed in the harvest of

sea life that Lencho had finally captured: sea spiders, starfish, coral formations, fans, limpets, snails, a giant rock scallop and a porcupine fish, which the Acapulco boys called blowfish because they gulped water and swelled up like balloons when molested or captured.

Tony started the boat while Lencho set to work, industriously cleaning the coral and scraping the shells of various kinds to make souvenirs for the tourists. He talked volubly all the time he was doing it and his audience obviously enjoyed his chatter. He did not speak English as well as Tony but the tourists seemed to like that, too, and Tony privately thought that Lencho occasionally mispronounced words for effect.

Deliberately, he closed his eyes and ears to his immediate surroundings and looked at the glittering open sea beyond the bay, wishing with all his heart that he were out there—all alone—in a boat of his own. The longing was so intense that it was almost like a physical pain.

A few minutes later they chugged into Caletilla and Tony beached the *Pelicano*. Dropping into the water, he and Lencho pushed the launch far enough onto the sand so the tourists would not get their feet wet.

"It's been so interesting," said one of the elderly ladies as Lencho helped her gallantly over the stern, onto the wooden step, and thence to the beach. "I'd like you to have—" She pressed a bill into Lencho's hand.

He bowed and smiled his thanks, without saying anything, and Tony caught a flick of hard black eyes turned in his direction.

He hopes I didn't see what she gave him, he thought

as he continued handing the passengers ashore, courteously but without comment.

The auburn-haired girl was last. She accepted Lencho's outstretched hand but when she turned and smiled, she was looking at Tony.

"Thank you for a nice trip," she murmured.

Lencho watched her as she walked away and then turned to Tony, scowling. "If she goes with us again, you lay off!" he ordered roughly.

"I haven't done anything to attract her attention and I'm not interested in her," Tony answered curtly. "I can't help it if she smiles at me! What did the little gray-haired lady give you?"

Lencho's black eyes narrowed. "Ten pesos," he said reluctantly. "But I earned it, bursting my lungs to get that blowfish!"

"Okay, keep it." Tony shrugged. All tips were supposed to be split fifty-fifty but he knew that if he argued with Lencho right then, his smoldering anger would burst into flame.

He took a little package of tortilla-wrapped beans from under the stern bench. "Meet you here at three o'clock, after lunch?"

"Yes. And this time see if you can get at least five passengers. I got eight of the eleven we just took." Lencho's voice was cold.

Tony bit back the retort on his tongue and walked down the beach without answering. He hated Lencho; he hated himself; he hated everyone on the beach. . . .

Everyone but Julio, he corrected himself, lengthening

his stride in the direction of the restaurant on Caletilla where his friend worked. He felt he had to see Julio for a moment—now—and listen to some of his hard common sense, or he'd never be able to get through the rest of the day!

6

Ruled Off the Beach

Julio was busy cleaning fish at his outdoor stand. He looked up as Tony approached and signaled, by putting his thumb and forefinger close together, that he would be through in a little minute.

Tony nodded and dropped into one of the chairs at the outdoor tables. He ordered a limeade from a passing waiter and opened his package of food. But he was in no hurry to eat. He sat leaning his forehead on the palms of his hands.

"*Qué te pasa, amigo?*" Julio dropped into the chair beside him. "What's the matter? You look very sad. Is it Lencho?"

"Partly." Tony's sigh came up from his bare toes. "What is there about that boy that makes one want to kill him?"

Julio grinned in spite of himself. "His arrogance, of course. You are the first to stand him this long. I hear by the grapevine that Captain García is very pleased at the way you work together."

Tony grimaced. "But not pleased enough to raise my pay, I suppose."

"It wouldn't be much, anyway. How are the tips now, Tony? Beginning the middle of December, more people come down. You should make a little more, soon."

"He keeps more than his share," Tony said grimly, downing his iced limeade in one gulp, hoping it would cool his anger. "And I let him keep it for two reasons. One, it is true that he gets more clients than I do. I hate to drum up trade. The other reason is that I know if we start to really argue, I will haul off and hit him!"

"Maybe somebody on one of the other boats will quit," Julio suggested without much hope. At the beginning of the good part of the season, it was unlikely.

"I'm not sure—" Tony began.

Just then one of the waitresses called Julio and he hurried off to prepare a coconut, whacking away at the outside green fiber and expertly chopping a small hole in the top. When he returned, he brought Tony three opened clams and a piece of fried fish on a plate.

"To go with the tortillas," he said.

"Thank you, my friend." Tony picked at his food and went on, "I'm not sure that another boat would be much better. The truth is I'm just not cut out for this business, Julio. I hate putting on shows for people. The whole thing seems phony to me."

"*Caramba,* I don't see why!" Julio remonstrated. "You're selling something the tourists want—the same as I am when I put a plate of oysters in front of them. It's no disgrace to sell your knowledge of the sea—and your ability to dive—to people who want it!"

Tony turned the empty glass around in his fingers, looking at it with absent, troubled eyes. "I hate the whole mad scramble for money," he muttered. "It's disgusting."

"Everybody has to work at making money, Tony!"

"I'm willing to work, to earn my living, to help Marta, to satisfy my uncle," Tony said slowly. "But I'd like it to be honest, simple, dignified work—like my father used to do. There's something false about all this."

Julio shook his head. "You're an idealist, my friend."

Tony didn't answer for a moment and then he said, "You remember that tame bear we saw downtown last year, on our way home from school? With its leg chained to its owner? The man said 'March!' and then 'Lie down!' and then 'Dance!' And afterward he gave the bear his hat to take up a collection. I feel just like that bear."

"Oh, come now!" Julio protested, laughing.

"Exactly like that bear," Tony insisted. "It wouldn't be quite so bad if somebody else took up the collection. You know I love to dive. If I could take out one or two people, I'd dive for them all day and tell them everything I know about the fish and the sea, for pleasure. But doing it for a crowd—making a rehearsed show out of it—doing it to get as much money as can be squeezed out of them —*I hate it!* I—"

He broke off and Julio followed his glance. The auburn-haired girl was walking by the table. Tony nodded to her stiffly and was silent until she was out of earshot.

Julio raised his eyebrows.

"A passenger," Tony explained wearily. "Another bone of contention between Lencho and me. He fancies himself a conquistador of all females, as you know, and she isn't paying him enough attention." He pushed back his chair. "Well, I've got to dance up and down the beach now," he said grimly, "getting customers for the next trip."

"It isn't two-thirty yet," Julio remonstrated. "They're all eating or taking a siesta. Rest a moment, *hombre!*"

Tony hesitated and then relaxed into his chair again. "I don't know what I'd do without you and Pedro," he said quietly.

"Where is Pedro, by the way? I haven't seen him for several days now."

"His father took him to Taxco last week. They were supposed to return yesterday." Tony's voice was a little worried. "I hope his father doesn't like Taxco better and decide to stay there."

"He won't. Not if Pedro has anything to say about it! I never saw a boy so crazy about Acapulco—except you." Julio smiled. "He's a little scrawny, your gringo friend, but he has a good head on his shoulders."

"A good heart, too," Tony added. "He is a good boy. Almost too good. He trusts everyone. He thinks everyone is as generous and honest as he is. He loves Acapulco but he has really seen only the surface of it—the smiles, the eternal sun, the gay songs. He hasn't seen the treacherous side. Acapulco has two faces, like the ocean. One soft and peaceful and easygoing; the other—murderous. The big fish chase the little fish on land as well as in the sea."

"*Vaya!*" Julio mocked. "How philosophical you are becoming, brother! I take it back—you are a realist, after all."

"Yes," Tony said soberly. "I love Acapulco and I love the sea, but I know that neither of them can be trusted."

"Speaking of the sea, what about the fishing, Tony? Didn't you tell me a while back that you were going to take Pedrito out fishing in the deep water?"

"Yes, I did." For the first time that day, Tony really smiled. "We went night fishing with Don Clemente about two weeks ago. *Ayee*, what a wonderful night that was, Julio! The darkness, and the silence, and the big stars, and the lights streaming across the bay. Such peace! You feel in another world. Pedro decided then and there that he would be a fisherman, too."

"Well?" Julio demanded. "Why don't you go oftener? Earn extra money?"

"That was the idea," Tony said sadly. "But in the first place, Don Clemente already has a partner—his nephew. In the second place, the catch was poor, very poor. But the worst thing was that I found I could not fish all night and dive all day. I was falling asleep while I talked to the tourists. Unfortunately for me, the glass-bottomed boat pays better than the fishing."

"What does the Señor Carson think about all these excursions Pedro takes with you?" Julio's voice was curious.

"Pedro's father is a strange person," Tony said thoughtfully. "Rather absent-minded. I have seen him only twice, but I have the impression, from what Pedro says, that he also is a too-innocent person, though he has been around a lot and was a newspaper reporter. He said that he trusted Pedro with me—"

"And why not?" Julio asked, surprised.

Tony shook his head. "He should not trust anyone on sight, like that."

"You know, Tony," Julio said kindly, "this deal with Lencho is making you cynical. What you need is a change. A neighbor of ours is giving a fiesta, day after tomorrow. Why don't you come? A little music and good company will put new life in you."

Tony smiled gratefully but he shook his head again. "I'm dog tired when night comes," he confessed ruefully. "I better not, this time. But thanks, anyway. Now I really must be off. It's late."

"Take it easy," Julio called after him. "It isn't a matter of life and death, you know—this job."

But Tony had forgotten how to take things easy. To him, this job and making money toward a launch *was* a matter of life and death.

When he left the beach that afternoon after three more trips, he was exhausted and frustrated and nervous.

To one side of the beach there was a small hidden spot surrounded by high rocks, where he and Lencho sometimes cached small objects overnight so they would not be stolen from the boat. Peter had occasionally waited for Tony there, after the trips were over in the afternoon, and as Tony approached the place now, to leave his spear and extra bathing trunks, he found himself hoping that his friend had returned from Taxco and would be waiting for him today.

But it was not Peter who was behind the rocks. As Tony neared the spot, he suddenly heard a girl's voice saying furiously in English, "Let me go! How dare you!" Then the sound of a slap.

In a split second, Tony had scrambled around the crevice. Lencho, with an arrogant smile on his face, was holding the struggling, auburn-haired girl in his arms and was trying to kiss her.

Tony rushed Lencho, hauling him bodily away from the girl and hurling him against the rock wall. "Get out of here!" he commanded the girl through clenched teeth. "Run!"

She backed off, her gray eyes wide, but Tony did not see whether or not she left because Lencho was coming at him, his small eyes glittering with fury.

"I told you not to interfere in my business!" he growled. Tony didn't bother to answer. He swung at the threatening eyes, the set lips. Lencho dodged and caught the blow on his ear, then lashed his own fist out like a sledge hammer and landed a wind-cutting blow on Tony's chest.

Half turned by the impact, Tony caught a glimpse of a bleached yellow head bearing down on them and he groaned inwardly. Peter had returned, all right—at the wrong moment. "Pedro, go back!" he yelled. "Don't get mixed up in this. Go back!"

But Peter had already plowed in, trying to wedge his thin body between the two angry boys and separate them. A stunning blow, intended for Tony, caught him full on the back of the head and he went down like a stone.

Red rage blinded Tony. At the beginning of the fight, he had intended only to engage Lencho's attention until the girl had escaped. But now, with his friend knocked out and perhaps seriously hurt, all the frustrations and swallowed insults of the last month suddenly welled up in him. Fury possessed him and he began to fight in deadly earnest.

His fist smashed into Lencho's nose and he could feel the cracking of the bone. Within a second, a retaliating blow to his eye made him stagger back, blindly shaking his head. Lencho followed up his advantage, charging like a bull toward Tony's solar plexus, but the boy wheeled just in time, half falling over a boulder as he did so. Lencho was on him at once, his hand at Tony's throat and his right fist raised. Tony jerked his knees up violently, catapulting the other boy off to one side.

Both were on their feet instantly. Tony moved in swiftly and swung at Lencho's jaw with a force that made his knuckles ache. Lencho staggered back, snarling with rage, and at that moment, Tony suddenly felt his arms seized from behind in an iron grip.

Thinking it was one of the other beach boys, he struggled angrily to free himself. It was against all the unwritten laws—interfering in a fight between two evenly matched men. But as he twisted and turned, he saw that the man who held him was in police uniform and that another policeman had a strangle hold on Lencho.

He heard a voice of authority behind him: "Knock them both over the head and put them in jail! Bring the gringo, too. They're all ruled off the beach for good!"

With his arms pinioned behind him, unable to move, Tony saw the billy descending on his head at the same moment that he heard the girl's shrill scream.

7

Behind Bars

WHEN TONY RECOVERED CONSCIOUSNESS, HE WAS LYING ON a cold cement floor, in almost complete darkness. His throat was dry and his head ached furiously. It throbbed even more as he moved to examine his surroundings so he lay still again, staring at a small patch of stars through a barred window high above his head.

Recollection flooded in. He was in jail. The fight with Lencho . . . the police . . . Pedro. . . .

Pedro! Where was he? Tony sat up too quickly and the stars outside the window seemed to come rocketing down through his head. He leaned back again, groaning softly. Pedro was not here, at any rate. Although Tony could not see much, he sensed that he was alone in the small cell.

He remembered the *gendarme* saying, "Bring the gringo, too." But perhaps they had taken Pedro home when they found out he was the son of a visiting American writer. Tony devoutly hoped so.

Hearing the scurrying sound of a rat, he lashed out with his arm and the noise receded. Thinking of the rats, lying flat became unbearable and he raised himself slowly, every muscle protesting, until he could lean his throbbing head against the wall.

That girl—that gray-eyed, auburn-haired American girl—was the cause of all this. For a moment Tony thought of her bitterly but then, because he was innately honest, he admitted to himself that he would have welcomed any excuse to fight Lencho.

However, if it hadn't been for the girl, they might have had it out in some less public spot where the police would not have interfered. Tony did not need to be told how the authorities frowned on beach brawls. It drew crowds and made a bad impression on the tourists. Sometimes it started feuds that went on and on interminably, even ending in murder.

But it was done now. He had fought and he would automatically lose his job, just at the beginning of the best part of the tourist season when he might *possibly* have been able to save more money toward a boat.

He was acutely uncomfortable from thirst, chill, his bruised body and his cut face. But it was mental pain that made him groan this time. He had wanted more than anything in the world to prove that he could earn the money necessary to stay in Acapulco. And this was the way he had done it—his first job over in five weeks and no way to get another, now, for months! Not on the beach, at least. The police and the boat owners had long memories.

When Uncle Juan knew about this, he would be more determined than ever to take him to Mexico City and start him on a hotel career.

Shivering with his thin-shirted back against the cold cement wall of the jail, he thought longingly of the clean, dark sea only a few blocks away, rocking peacefully in the moonlight. It was in another world from this dirty, smelly, rat-ridden jail.

This was the other side of Acapulco—the side he had been talking about to Julio just this afternoon—or was it yesterday afternoon? The side Pedro hadn't seen. Tony hoped he wasn't seeing it now, somewhere in another cell.

The merry-go-round of his thoughts made him feel more ill and thirsty than ever. He was about to try to stand and call the jailer, to ask for a drink of water, when he heard footsteps and then a light snapped on in the corridor outside.

"Tony Castillo!" The voice was brusque. "Visitors!"

Tony knew he had never in his life been so glad to see his sister Marta's slender, oval face and Aunt Raquel's plump one. He gave them a twisted grin of welcome and struggled to raise himself.

"Don't get up." Marta pushed him back gently. "You are really hurt, Tony!"

"It probably looks worse than it is." His voice was ragged from the dryness in his mouth. "The thirst is the worst part. That—and wondering about Pedro."

"We brought water." Aunt Raquel took a clay jar from her basket. "Pedro is all right. A little bump on his head. He's in the other part of the jail and his father is with him. You can thank Señor Carson that we are here—these stupid guards would not let us in, the first time we came. But Pedro's father bribed them well."

Marta was unwrapping other bundles from the basket. "*Tacos*," she said, "and some hot soup."

Relieved about Peter, Tony gulped from the bottle of water. "*Ayee,* that is good! What about Señor Carson— and Uncle Juan? I suppose they're both angry with me?"

"I do not understand Americans," Aunt Raquel said shortly. "As for your uncle, he doesn't know about this yet. He was busy in the store when Julio brought us word of the fight. Later, he had a business appointment in town."

Tony sighed. They were trying to protect him but of course Uncle Juan would know, sooner or later. News traveled fast in Acapulco.

"Eat, brother," Marta urged. "You must be starved. It's almost eleven o'clock."

"Is that all? I thought it was nearly morning!"

Tony had not been conscious of hunger but with the odor of the hot soup, he realized he was ravenous. When he had finished all they had brought, he felt restored in body and soul, despite his cuts and bruises.

He looked up to find his aunt studying him with her button-black eyes.

"We saw Lencho, too," she said abruptly. "His nose is broken. It was a mistake, Tony—that fight."

"I know," he muttered. "But he asked for it."

"We've heard all about it. Nevertheless, it was a mistake, my boy. Lencho won't forget."

"I'm not as worried about that as I am about the job," Tony said grimly. "Now I'll have to find something else—and something that pays more."

"Well, don't think about it now." His aunt's voice was

more gentle. "Sleep if you can. You'll be called before the judge in the morning."

"We brought a sarape," Marta added. "This place is cold and damp. Julio told us."

"*Gracias,* both of you." Tony was sincerely grateful. He felt he didn't deserve so much consideration.

"One of us will be here in the morning," Aunt Raquel said. "Good luck, *mi hijito.* I'm glad we find you in one piece, at least!"

They had barely gone when the surly guard was back again, this time with Peter's father.

"Well, Tony," the American said, peering down at him, "you look a little banged up!"

"Mr. Carson, I am sorry," Tony said contritely, in English. "About Peter, I mean."

"It wasn't your fault he mixed in." Mr. Carson looked very tall and white-skinned in the dim light. And very out of place. Tony wondered if the *Norteamericano* had ever been in a jail before. Certainly not in one like this!

"Pete told me about it," Mr. Carson went on. "He says you warned him to keep away."

"I—"

"I'm glad he got into it," Mr. Carson said in a tone of calm satisfaction.

"You are what?" Tony was dumfounded.

"Why not? I wouldn't want Peter to be a coward, or disloyal to his friends. You are his friend, Tony."

"Maybe I shouldn't be," Tony muttered. "I only get him in trouble."

"We'll risk it." Mr. Carson smiled a little. "Is there anything I can do for you, my boy?"

"No, sir. You already have, getting my aunt and sister in here."

"It was nothing. I'll be going, then. They are letting Pete come home with me. I convinced the police that he was more or less a bystander in your argument."

"Good. I'm glad he can go," Tony said earnestly.

"Good night, then, *muchacho*. Rest now. *Hasta mañana.*"

"Good night, Mr. Carson—and many thanks."

What a nice person Peter's father is! Tony thought. If all gringos were like that. . . .

Left alone again, Tony wrapped himself in the wool sarape, warmed and comforted. It was amazing how much less hopeless things looked, given a full stomach and a few kind words.

But he slept fitfully, with vivid dreams that were almost nightmares. And he wakened early, watching the brightening sky beyond his barred window and worrying about his problems again.

It was the middle of the afternoon when the two boys were finally called before the judge. Lencho, already in the office, glowered when Tony was escorted in. But Tony forgot his enemy when he saw the auburn-haired girl, neatly attired in a blue cotton dress sitting at one side of the room with Peter Carson. Peter grinned at Tony and surreptitiously made a circle of his thumb and forefinger as a sign of encouragement.

The informal hearing was brief. Both boys pleaded guilty to fighting on the beach and disturbing the peace.

Lencho's attempt to justify himself was cut short by the judge, who asked the girl, through an interpreter, for her version.

She answered quietly that Lencho had stopped her as she was leaving the beach, saying that he had an unusual shell he wanted to give her for a souvenir. Then, within the circle of the rocks, he had tried forcibly to kiss her. She had slapped him and screamed, and Tony had appeared and fought with Lencho.

She added in a straightforward manner that she felt responsible for the whole matter and hoped that the judge would be lenient with both boys, under the circumstances.

The judge sighed. "There are often misunderstandings here because American girls are brought up differently from Mexican girls," he said. "They mix more with the opposite sex and have more freedom. But *these* boys should understand this, because they have been around tourists long enough." He looked at Lencho sternly.

"I thought she wanted to be kissed," Lencho muttered sullenly.

"Well, perhaps after a few days' leisure in jail you'll remember, next time, to ask whether a girl wants to be kissed," the judge said curtly. "In addition to three days of confinement, you are prohibited from work with tourists for the rest of the season."

Lencho's face was black with anger. "Tony doesn't try half as hard to please the tourists as I do!" he blurted out. "He hates them! I've done nine tenths of the work on our boat, for the last five weeks."

Tony's ears turned red and he avoided looking at the girl. "I don't hate them," he said gruffly. "It's just—I don't know what to say to them. I'd rather work by myself."

"Then perhaps you'd better find some other job where you'll be able to work by yourself," the judge said in a cool voice. "You also are forbidden tourist work for the remainder of the season. Case dismissed."

Tony knew from the look Lencho gave him, as he went off with the guard, that the matter was not ended. Once Lencho was out of jail, he'd get even. But Tony couldn't worry about that right now. He was relieved that there had been no fine or imprisonment for him, to make the whole matter worse. It was bad enough to be forbidden to work on the beach!

"They wouldn't let me testify because I was involved in it," Peter whispered to Tony as they left the judge's office. "But I found the girl and got her to come. I thought that would be better."

"It was." Tony clapped a hand on his friend's shoulder. "You have just been promoted, Pedro. You are now my twin! You know what that means in Mexico? Even closer than brother."

Peter's grin was pleased.

As they emerged from the courthouse, they saw the girl walking slowly down the shady side of the street.

"She was sorry about this," Peter said. "She really is very nice, Tony."

"No doubt." Tony's voice was grim. "But I hope I never see her again!"

When he got home, late in the afternoon, it seemed to

him that he had been away a long, long time. In the city jail only one night—but the work on the glass-bottomed boat had kept him so busy that for over a month he had been at home only to eat and sleep.

Marta and their young cousins, Juanita and Lourdes, were taking care of the store, after the three-hour dinner and siesta lull. Uncle Juan was nowhere to be seen. Aunt Raquel came out of the kitchen wing as Tony stood hesitating in the middle of the patio.

"Clean yourself up," she said. "I heated a pail of water and I am warming your dinner. We've all eaten, long ago."

It was pleasant to be coddled, Tony thought. After he had given himself a thorough scrubbing to get rid of the jail dirt and smells and had eaten a strangely lonely meal at the corridor table, he stretched out in the hammock under the mango tree and slept for two solid hours.

When he wakened, refreshed, it was dusk. The sky was changing to colors of opal as the sun dropped behind the western mountains. Voices echoed from the store in front, but out here it was very peaceful. Bats circled in their crazy, aimless-looking twilight flight above the trees. Pancho Villa, the parrot, complained softly to himself in an almond tree.

Tony lay for a few minutes, unthinking, letting the peace and beauty of the evening sink into him. Then he locked his fingers under his head and began considering the possibilities. What now? What was he going to do next—tomorrow—to earn money?

After a while, he heard a door open behind him and a snapped-on light half illuminated the patio.

"Tony!"

The boy got up quickly and went to the veranda, where his uncle sat stiffly at the table. He never relaxes, Tony thought. Even when he's lying in a hammock, his body is stiff and controlled.

His uncle's amber eyes studied the partly closed eye and the swollen jaw. Tony waited for the tongue-lashing he fully expected.

But when Uncle Juan spoke, his voice was surprisingly quiet.

"You see, my boy, that you're not going to be able to do this—make a decent living alone in Acapulco? Are you ready now to give up this foolish idea and go to the city with us, as I want you to? Soon we won't be around, to get you out of scrapes like this one!"

Tony flushed, remembering how good it had been to see Aunt Raquel and Marta, bringing food and comfort to the jail. He would miss them, of course—all of them— and he felt as though he were being pulled in two by the conflict that waged in him. Yet underneath was the deep, clear certainty that he was right. He could *not* go to the city.

"Uncle Juan," he said unhappily, "as I've told you many times, I thank you for all you have done for me and Marta. But I *have* to stay here. Acapulco is my home—"

The amber eyes hardened. "Then I was mistaken. I thought this house was your home. I thought we were your family."

Tony had not cried since his father had died, six years before, but now he felt the sting of tears behind his eyelids. His shoulders slumped. How could he explain?

After a moment's silence, his uncle threw out his hands and dropped them to his sides in a gesture of hopelessness.

"Very well." The voice was cold and noncommittal again. "We will return to our original arrangement. If you have earned, by honest means, two thousand pesos by the end of January, you may stay here. If not, you go to the city with us."

Tony felt lonely and wretched as the shop door closed behind his uncle. But he was getting what he wanted—another chance.

For the next ten days, Tony worked harder than he had ever worked in his life. On two afternoons he was able to borrow a compressed-air tank from a friend and he spent the precious air time in hunting and raising an anchor which had been lost from one of the cruise boats.

But most of the time he had to skin dive from the surface, using only his diving mask, rubber flippers and his own lungs. He haunted the lesser-known coves and inlets around Acapulco in a frenzied search for seafood delicacies such as scallops, oysters and *percebes*—the iodine-loaded, fingerlike goose barnacles—taking them afterward to the restaurants on the coast boulevard, haggling to get the last possible centavo for them.

He advertised his availability and did every odd job that he could find to do, around the docks and the neighborhood, no matter how distasteful it was.

One long, backbreaking day, he worked at unloading cargo from a visiting Japanese boat, and he would have worked a second day, but the dock foreman shook his head.

"You're strong, Tony, for your age. But this is a man's job. I should never have let you keep at it all day yesterday."

Peter helped as much as he could, after school. On Saturday the two boys rented a paddle board and paddled around behind the island, on the sea side, to a cave where Tony knew there were oysters. Peter maneuvered the flat board skillfully in the waves, as Tony had taught him, keeping it in position off the rocks while Tony dived in water twenty feet deep, breaking the oysters away from the coral rock with an iron bar and coming up every couple of minutes for more air. It was strenuous work. He got five dozen that day, but at night he was so exhausted that he slept like a dead man for ten hours.

Hard work or not, he would have loved it all, if so much hadn't depended on the financial results. By the end of ten days, he knew that he was never going to be able to save the money he needed by that method of skin diving.

"I'm not getting enough, fast enough," he said to Peter as the two boys walked along the dock one afternoon. "To make money, you have to have a boat with a motor, or an aqualung, or better still—both."

Peter nodded in reluctant agreement. After a moment's pause, he said, "You know, Tony, what you need right now is a little diversion. You're going around in circles."

"Julio told me the same thing, the last day I worked on the glass-bottomed boat." Tony's voice was moody.

"I was wondering," Peter suggested tentatively, "if you'd come to the *posada* they're going to have at our boardinghouse tonight. This is the first night of the *posadas*, isn't it? I've never seen one, and you could explain it to me."

Tony stared at him. Pedro seemed so well adapted to Acapulco that sometimes Tony forgot what a relatively short time the American boy had lived in Mexico. "You mean you've *never* been to a *posada*, not even when you were in Guadalajara last winter?"

Peter shook his head. "We didn't know many people there," he said. "I've heard about the *posada* parties, of course, and I've read a little about them. But I'd sure like to see one, with somebody who knows. Dad would, too."

Peter was trying to sound casual, but Tony heard the wistful note in his voice, and suddenly he felt ashamed of himself. Peter had certainly been doing his best to help, and Mr. Carson had been more than kind in the jail. Maybe it was time he did something for them, for a change!

"Listen, Pedro," he said, trying to forget that he was tired and discouraged and in no mood for a party. "That boardinghouse *posada* may be all right, but then again it may be something just put on for tourists. Why don't you and your father come to our neighborhood fiesta, instead? It may not be elegant, but at least it will be genuine."

"But—but—we haven't been invited!" Peter stuttered, his eyes shining with sudden excitement.

"Well, I'm inviting you now. Anybody in the barrio

can invite his friends. They'd be glad to have you and your father. The more people, the more interesting it is."

"Gosh, Tony, I'd sure like that! Can we bring something?"

"You don't have to. But if it would make your father feel any better, you can bring some candy for the *piñatas*."

"The *piñatas*," Peter said uncertainly. "Are those the decorated things they dangle for kids to hit at?"

Tony looked at him in amazement. "You really don't know much about the Christmas fiestas, do you?"

It seemed incredible to him until he remembered how differently they celebrated Christmas in the United States. He hesitated for only a second before he spoke again. If he was going to introduce Peter and his father to their first Mexican Christmas party, he might as well do it right.

"Look, Pedro, if you don't even know much about *piñatas*, maybe you and your father would like to go with me to the market this evening and see the displays of the Christmas stuff. That way you'll get a better idea of what it's all about, before the party begins."

"Gee!" Peter breathed. "What time should we go? I'll run and tell Dad now."

"Let's leave around seven. The market's open late, and you can see all there is to see in an hour. Then we can go right from there to the fiesta."

"That would be perfect! You're sure you want to do this, Tony? I know you're pretty tired from the hard work you've been doing."

"Sure I want to do it." Tony's voice was hearty. He

was even beginning to get a little excited about it himself. He had seen many *posadas* in his sixteen years but it would be sort of fun to explain them to people who had never seen one. "I'm not really physically tired—just tired of thinking—and anyway, there's plenty of time for a siesta before we have to get ready. I'll pick you up at your boardinghouse around six-thirty. Okay?"

"Okay!" Peter echoed happily. "See you later!"

8

The *Posada*

WHEN TONY PRESENTED HIMSELF AT THE CARSONS' BOARD-
inghouse, late that afternoon, he was scrubbed and
dressed in blue trousers and a bright blue shirt which set
off his ruddy-brown skin to good advantage.

"*Hombre,* I hardly recognize you!" Peter grinned.

"Brother, I could say the same." Tony grinned back,
admiring Peter's white shirt and creased white slacks. "I
guess we've never seen each other so dressed up!"

"Tony, it's nice of you to do this," Mr. Carson said as
he appeared in the doorway. "It will be much more
interesting to see a *posada* in your neighborhood than
the one they've arranged for the boardinghouse guests."

"I'm glad you can come," Tony said, meaning it. "I
don't know why I didn't think of inviting you until Pedro
mentioned it."

While they walked to the market Tony explained in
his best English that *posada* meant lodging, and that the
first part of the fiesta was a ceremony in which the guests
act out the Bible story of how the Holy Family wandered
for nine nights, trying to find room in an inn.

"That's why the *posadas* are held for nine nights

before Christmas," he said. "Every night there's a fiesta in a different house, with everybody in the neighborhood cooperating."

"I've read about that," Mr. Carson nodded.

"But where do the *piñatas* fit into it?" Peter asked, puzzled.

"They don't fit into the first part," Tony told him. "There are two parts to a *posada*, Pedro. The first half is the ceremony—kind of solemn, and the second half is fun—the breaking of the *piñatas*. They're really thin clay jars decorated into all kinds of shapes with tissue paper and tinsel. You'll see some in a minute."

The labyrinthian Acapulco market, which covered several blocks, was full of color and excitement on this first night of the Christmas parties. The first section they came to was given over entirely to booths brimming with mountains of hard candy, nuts, dried fruits, and small but durable toys.

"These are the things they fill the *piñatas* with," Tony explained. "And there are the empty *piñatas*." He pointed to an array of large and beautifully made paper figures which swung on ropes above the street stands: ships, clowns, animals, airplanes and many other objects.

"Let's get one!" Mr. Carson said with sudden enthusiasm. "We'll take it to the party with us, along with the things to fill it. They can use an extra one, can't they, Tony?"

"They use as many as they can get. But you don't have to buy one. Nobody would expect you to," Tony protested, knowing that the *piñatas* were fairly costly and that Peter's father did not have much money. Collections were taken up for the neighborhood parties, so no great expense fell on any one person. But for Mr. Carson to buy one alone was a different matter.

"I haven't gotten a Christmas present for you yet, Pete." Mr. Carson looked at his son questioningly.

Peter nodded. "I'd rather have a *piñata* than anything else," he said emphatically.

"But if you take it to the party, *you* won't have it," Tony told him. "The kids will break it."

"I'll have the fun of watching it get broken," Peter insisted.

"Okay, if that's the way you want it," Tony surrendered, outwardly reluctant but inwardly pleased that his gringo friends were so interested in the Mexican traditions.

"Which one do you like best, Pete?" Mr. Carson turned to his son, his brown eyes almost as eager as Peter's blue ones.

The three of them finally decided on a realistic-looking bull with its head down, ready to charge. Then they bought enough bags of candy and small gifts to more than fill it.

After that, Tony led them to a section of the market where the booths were given over to the small figurines and trimmings used for the construction of the manger scenes.

"What a lot of work must have gone into these!" Mr. Carson mused, picking up a three-inch clay figure of a peasant with a bundle of kindling on his back. "Look how perfectly he's made, Pete—even to the creases in his hat and the buckles on his sandals. They'd make good drawing models for you."

"Aunt Raquel and the girls arranged our *nacimiento* yesterday—that's what we call the manger scenes here," Tony remarked.

"Does every family have one, Tony?" Peter asked. "Must be kind of expensive."

"Well, they're used year after year, you see," Tony answered. "People start with just the most important pieces, and then they add one or two figures whenever they can."

It was well after eight o'clock by the time Peter and his father were able to tear themselves away from the fascinations of the pre-Christmas market.

"It's still early for the fiesta to start," Tony said as they walked back through town. "I'll show you one of the best *nacimientos* around our neighborhood, on the way back."

"Don't they mind people coming in to stare?" Peter asked.

"Of course not," Tony assured him. "They're glad to show it. After all, they've put a lot of work into it and they like to have it appreciated!"

A few minutes later, they stopped at the door of a high-walled house and after Tony had knocked and introduced his friends to the señora, the three of them were ushered to a sheltered part of the huge patio where the *nacimiento* had been set up.

Peter and his father stood in front of it for a long time, admiring the beauty of the scene and the ingenuity displayed in its arrangement.

It was after nine o'clock when they arrived at the home of Tony's neighbor, where the *posada* was being held. The huge patio was already filled with people, young and old.

Tony courteously presented the Carsons to their hosts and then led them to his own family. Although Mr. Carson's Spanish was much less fluent than Peter's, he managed to chat at some length with Uncle Juan and Aunt Raquel. Tony and Peter drifted away toward a group of boys their own age.

"I've often seen Marta, of course, when I called for you at home," Peter murmured in Tony's ear, "and I always thought she was pretty. But tonight she's absolutely beautiful!"

Tony, pleased, glanced back at his sister. He himself thought that Marta was the prettiest girl at the party, but it was nice to have Peter confirm his opinion.

Tony was about to say something when he felt a hearty clap on his shoulder and turned to find Julio beside him, grinning broadly.

"Julio! *Qué bueno!* I didn't know you were coming to this *posada!*"

"I came, hoping you'd be here, though I didn't really expect you to be! *Hola*, Pedro, how goes it?"

"Fine." Peter smiled and shook hands.

"Looks as though I got here just in time," Julio remarked, nodding to the other side of the patio, where their hostess was beginning to organize the procession.

"Yes," Tony said. "We'll leave you for a while now, Julio. I'm going to pair up with Pedro, so I can explain things to him. He's never been to a *posada* before."

"You don't mean it!" The older boy sounded shocked. "Pedro, I can see you still have a long way to go before becoming a real Mexican! Take care of him, Tony. I'll see you later. Maybe they'll let me walk in the procession with Marta or some other pretty girl—"

"He's just joking," Tony told Peter as they took their places in the procession. "Girls and boys don't mix for this part of the *posada*. Not until later."

Peter watched the proceedings with interest. The guests, well accustomed to the traditional order of things, had lined up in pairs. Children were in front, with two of the youngest carrying a small platform with the figures of Mary on a burro, Joseph following behind, and a guiding angel hovering over them. Each guest was supplied with a tall lighted candle.

When they were ready, the electric lights were extinguished, and the column of candles began to move slowly from one patio door to another.

"They go to nine doors, representing the nine nights," Tony whispered to Peter.

At each door they stopped and sang the traditional song which Tony translated in a low voice for the benefit of Mr. Carson, who was just behind the two boys:

> In the name of heaven
> I beg you shelter. . . .

From the other side of the door, came the answer:

> This is no inn,
> Continue farther. . . .

The line of pilgrims went on from door to door, while

the impressive half-song, half-chant filled the patio and the entire neighborhood.

When they reached the ninth door, it was flung open and the procession of people entered, singing a hymn of joy and thanks, and placing their candles in front of the *nacimiento*.

"A beautiful custom," Mr. Carson said to Tony, obviously moved by the ceremony.

As the guests crowded back into the patio, they began to mix more freely and the scene became more animated.

"Now the second part of the fiesta begins," Tony explained to the Carsons. "The fun part. See, they're lowering the first *piñata*."

A gorgeous silver star, with blue paper tassels hanging from every point, dangled in the patio on a rope stretched between two young men who stood precariously on the low tile rooftops.

Peter and his father joined the circle of spectators and watched with interest as the first child was blindfolded, given a long stick, turned round and round to confuse him, then pushed in the general direction of the star.

The youngster pounded the air vigorously, but the star bobbed up and down, just out of reach, pulled to safety by the boys who were operating the ropes.

"They don't let it be hit right away," Tony explained, "so more children will have a chance to try."

It was one of the smallest girls who finally managed a blow that shattered the star and, from its horn of plenty goodies poured over the shrieking young guests as they all scrambled for their share.

After two other, smaller, *piñatas* had been broken by

the children, Mr. Carson's big charging bull was lowered into the patio and was greeted with applause and shouts of approval.

Their hostess held up her hand for silence.

"This *piñata*," she said, smiling, "was contributed by our American guests and it's for the young people, not the children. We'll give Pedro Carson, Tony's friend, a chance to break it first!"

Another wave of applause broke out as Peter, surprised, pleased and a little embarrassed, was pushed forward and blindfolded. After a few futile whacks, he pulled off the blindfold, laughing, and gave up.

"You didn't really try to break it, did you, Pedro?" Tony said to him, as Julio was pushed up to take his turn. "They gave you a chance to."

"No," Peter whispered back. "I want to see someone else break it. I wish it could be your sister Marta."

Tony slipped away and held a low conversation with one of the boys on the rooftop, who nodded and signaled to the other boy.

When Marta's turn came, they deliberately dangled the *piñata* in front of her. Although she was not trying very hard, the bull shattered with a light stroke of her stick—and Peter's wish was fulfilled. He smiled his thanks at Tony.

It was after eleven o'clock when supper was served, buffet style, since there were far too many guests to be seated all at once. There was turkey and pork and chicken, along with tortillas and beans, and the special colorful Christmas salad of oranges, bananas, peanuts, beets, sugar cane and several other ingredients.

While they were eating, a small orchestra began to play in one corner of the patio, and the young people paired off to dance. Marta and Julio were among the first couples on the floor. Tony watched them, thinking how fine it would be if Marta and his adopted family could remain in Acapulco.

"I wish things would stay the way they are," he said abruptly to Peter.

Peter, absorbed in the details of the fiesta, looked blank for a moment. Then, following Tony's eyes to Marta, he followed his thoughts, too.

"Nothing ever stays the same for long," he said soberly. "Everything's always changing, all the time. And I guess that getting used to the changes is part of growing up."

Tony stared and then laughed a little. "You know, Pedro, you look younger than you are—but sometimes you sure *sound* old. Real old!" He changed the subject, "Tell me, did you like the party?"

Peter became his own age again. "Tony, it was swell! I don't know how to thank you for bringing us!"

"That goes for me, too," said Mr. Carson, who was just then approaching the boys. "It was a fine experience, Tony, and I'm certainly grateful. I think I'd better get on home now. If you boys want to stay, I imagine you'll see that Pete gets home all right, Tony?"

"I think I ought to get some sleep, too." Tony looked at Peter questioningly. "From now on, the party is just dancing. Do you want to stay, Pedro? Julio would walk back to the boardinghouse with you, if you do. He always stays late."

"No, I'll go along with Dad," Peter said. "I'm not interested in the dancing. It was a wonderful evening, Tony! See you tomorrow?"

"*Seguro!*" Tony assured him. "But don't say good-by yet. I'll walk home with both of you, if you're going now."

9

Too Deep, Too Long

PETER HAD BEEN RIGHT, TONY THOUGHT WHEN HE WOKE
up the morning after the fiesta. The evening of entertainment had brushed some of the cobwebs from his
brain. He felt refreshed and invigorated, and when the
two boys met on the docks, early that afternoon, there
was new determination on Tony's face.

"I think I should try to get more commercial skin-
diving work," he told his friend resolutely. "A lot of
stuff goes to the bottom of this bay and isn't ever recovered. If I were sure of the jobs, I could afford to rent
an aqualung and—"

"What about sunken ships?" Peter interrupted eagerly.
"Maybe treasure ships?"

Tony smiled a little. "Ships have gone down in the
bay, Pedro," he conceded, "but long before this, they've
been stripped of whatever 'treasure' they may have had.
And bringing up the ship itself, even after it's been
taken to pieces, is a job for a salvage company. No, I
meant more practical stuff, like the anchor I raised the
other day. Most of the skin divers here won't be bothered
with those jobs because they can make more by giving

lessons to tourists. I just have to think of some good way to advertise my services."

The two boys stood in silence a moment, thinking about it as they watched the usual afternoon return of the fishing cruisers. Most of the boats flew red and navy flags on their riggers, indicating that they had caught sailfish, but Tony noticed the approach of one launch that had all its flags flying.

"They must have caught a big marlin," he said absently.

Sailfish were fairly plentiful in Acapulco waters, but marlin were more scarce. A catch of a three- or four-hundred-pound marlin was an event signaled to shore with all the flags a fishing launch possessed.

As the boat came closer, they could see the huge fish draped across the bow.

"It really is a whopper!" Peter exclaimed.

Tony noticed that the American tourist who jumped out when the boat docked did not look as happy as he should after fishing such a prize.

"If only my watch hadn't dropped overboard!" the man was lamenting. "I wouldn't have lost that for anything!"

"We could send a diver down to look for it," the launch captain said reluctantly, "but it's pretty deep out there."

"I'd pay well," the big American said. "It isn't the intrinsic value of the watch, you understand. My wife gave it to me on our twentieth wedding anniversary and —well, she has passed away since then. I wouldn't have traded it for a marlin twice this size!"

Tony, who had been listening intently, shot a quick

look at Peter. This was the kind of work he'd just been talking about! He broke into the conversation.

"Where was the watch lost?" he asked the captain.

"Oh, way out there, about a mile beyond Elephant Rock," the man muttered. "That water is twenty or thirty fathoms deep!"

Tony hesitated. He had never gone down as far as a hundred and twenty feet. On the occasions when he had had the use of an aqualung, he had never wanted to use the precious time that way. At such a depth, part of the time underwater had to be utilized in a slow ascent, in order to decompress properly and avoid the "bends"— a painful, crippling—and sometimes fatal—affliction of divers.

But if he found the watch quickly, there would be time enough. *Nothing ventured, nothing gained!* he thought.

"There are rock ledges in some places out there," he said aloud. "It might have fallen on one of those, which would make it simpler to find. Anyhow, I'd like to try."

"It's up to you." The captain shrugged.

"I'm a skin diver, sir," Tony told the American, in English. "If you like, I'll try to find your watch for you. But you'll have to rent a tank of compressed air for me to use."

"Of course!" The man turned to him eagerly. "I'll rent anything you need. And I'll pay you twenty dollars if you find it!"

Tony's eyes sparkled. Twenty dollars was a ridiculously high price for recovering a watch, but if it meant that much to this rich American, he would certainly do his level best to earn it! Twenty dollars was two hundred and fifty pesos. What a boost that would give his savings!

Within half an hour the tourist, Mr. Williams, had rented aqualung equipment and hired a speedboat to take them to the spot where the watch band had snapped and the watch had gone overboard, during his struggle with the marlin. The launch captain checked the position as carefully as possible.

"This is as close as I can come to it," he said finally.

Tony nodded and started to get into his diving gear.

"I wish I were going down with you," Peter said in a low voice.

"Next time." Tony smiled at him. He was heartily glad that Peter *wasn't* going down. He hadn't nearly enough experience to go so deep, and besides, Tony wanted to be single-minded for this job.

He dropped into the water quietly and finned straight down, exerting himself as little as possible and breathing lightly, in order to conserve the air. When his ears began to hurt, he hesitated for a minute, swallowing his saliva, and then continued.

After stopping several times to get rid of the pain in his ears, he knew that he must be about ninety feet down and he began to look for the rock ledges which he had hoped to find along here. Visibility was more limited now. The water was like green dusk. Swarms of small fish were hovering around him curiously.

But there were no rock ledges. Either his memory of other skin divers' stories had betrayed him—or they were mistaken.

There was nothing to do but keep on descending. The

water was colder now and the pressure on his ears was getting painful, in spite of his swallowing. Deeper and deeper. . . . The water was purple now, like evening sky. His hand in front of his mask was the dead color of putty.

Tony had never been so deep before and he began to feel a strange exhilaration. The shadow of an enormous fish hovered just on the fringe of the purple curtain that surrounded him. He waved his hand at it airily and it disappeared.

Then, suddenly, he was on the bottom. He felt a thrill of triumph. It was surely at least a hundred and sixty feet deep here! He wished that he had asked Mr. Williams to rent a depth gauge and a waterproof watch, along with the other equipment. This odd feeling of exhilaration and dreaminess, which came from being in such deep water, was going to make it difficult to judge the time.

However, it was too late to worry about that now. The main thing was to find the American's watch—quickly. Tony began finning slowly along the bottom, barely moving his feet, breathing as lightly as he could. In shallower water it would have been easy to see the watch at some distance. It would shine brightly in the refracted sunlight. But down in this purple twilight it was going to be harder.

He went in ever-widening circles, searching. He had just completed his fourth circle when he became aware of a long, dark silhouette sliding silently past him. A shark! He froze for a moment and it disappeared from sight.

He was on his sixth circle when he suddenly saw a gleam on the bottom and a moment later, he triumphantly held Mr. Williams' wrist watch in his hand. He had earned two hundred and fifty pesos!

But his gloating was short-lived. Just as he was about to rise—slowly, because at that depth he knew he would have to pause for frequent periods of decompression—he saw the long form again. It looked enormous, the triangular fin on its back standing up like a sail. Tony had never seen a shark as big as this, and he did not know what kind it was nor how dangerous it might be. It appeared to be at least fifteen feet long. He hesitated for a moment, praying that the monster would go away and leave him in peace. He didn't have time to hang around down here until the animal's curiosity was satisfied!

It disappeared for a moment and then it was there again, swimming slowly, silently, toward him. It swerved and passed in front of him, so close that he could see the small, hard-looking eyes and the white belly with three small fish hanging from it.

Hardly breathing at all, Tony rose slowly while the shark was going away from him, and stayed motionless as it came back, its huge blue body sliding past again, eying him.

Tony would not have been frightened except that he knew he had been under the water for some time. His air wouldn't hold out much longer. And he didn't dare fin up fast, for fear his dangling, wiggling legs would tempt the shark to pursue. It looked quite capable of swallowing him whole, in one gulp!

He hovered motionless, waiting. At one point, the

beast seemed to have gone for good and Tony rose several feet, as fast as he dared. But then it was there once more, passing over him at arm's length. Just as it had disappeared into the blue again, Tony choked. His air was gone! He groped hurriedly for the lever of the reserve air supply and opened it.

He had only a few minutes left.

He rose again, finning more rapidly, and watching on all sides. For the moment, the shark was nowhere in sight. If it came back, there was only one thing to do—pull his knife. He didn't want to do it, because it was impossible to tell how a shark was going to react to the pin prick of a knife in its tough skin. Sometimes it frightened them off, and sometimes it angered them into attack. But he'd have to risk it, because there wasn't any time left. He looked at the silver mist of the surface longingly.

The shark came back.

Tony shifted the watch to his left hand and reached for the knife in his belt with his right, moving as slowly as possible. When the huge form slid past again, he swiftly stabbed the white belly as hard as he could.

It was as though there was a terrific explosion in the water. Tony turned head over heels several times in a whirlpool of violent currents. By the time the bubbles cleared and he had found his sense of direction again, the shark was nowhere in sight but Tony himself was breathing hard—much too fast. He knew that what had hit him was the backwash from the huge creature's tail. He wasn't hurt—but precious time and air had been spent.

He went on up quickly, not hovering, now, for the required periods of decompression.

His reserve air gave out many feet from the surface. He pulled the quick release on his weight belt and felt it drop away. Tearing off his face mask, he let himself exhale slowly as he rose, fighting against panic and the impulse to keep the little remaining air in his lungs—which would have been fatal, he knew.

By the time his head broke the water, his lungs felt ready to burst. There was a great roaring in his ears. Only half conscious, he gulped the blessed air and went down again, pulled under by the weight of the tank. He had just time to see that the boat was a good fifty feet away—too far!

I'm going to drown, Tony thought dimly but with absolute certainty.

Yet when that lungful of air was gone, he instinctively pushed himself up again, with the last of his strength—and the boat was there and many hands were hauling him into it.

From a long way off, he heard someone say, "Look, his skin is turning blue! He's going to have the bends, sure. We'll have to get him to the recompression chamber—quick!"

Then everything went black and Tony heard no more.

10

Night Fishing

"AND REMEMBER—ABSOLUTELY *no* SKIN DIVING FOR AT least two months!" the doctor warned. "After that, we'll see."

"But I'm all right now!" Tony protested desperately, trying to convince himself that it was true. His joints still ached and he was rather dizzy, but that would wear off, surely. "I *have* to dive, to earn money!"

"You heard me." The doctor snapped his black bag shut and walked to the door of the skin-diving station where Tony had just spent six hours in the recompression chamber. "I won't be responsible if you go underwater again for several weeks. Come around to my office then, and we'll check you over."

He left the station without waiting for an answer, and Tony watched him go with somber eyes.

"I'm mighty sorry about this, boy." Mr. Williams broke the silence. The American had been in and out all afternoon, waiting to see the outcome of Tony's attack of the bends. "I feel as though it's all my fault."

"No," Tony said slowly, trying to be fair in spite of his

disappointment. "I was stupid not to realize that I might need two tanks of air, instead of one."

Naturally he had known all along that it would be safer to take two tanks. But he had figured that if he saved Mr. Williams money on the equipment, the man would more willingly pay the twenty dollars he had offered for the job.

"If I'd had two tanks," he went on aloud, "there would have been plenty of time, even with the shark bothering me."

Peter, who had stayed with Tony all afternoon, shivered at the mention of the shark.

"I shouldn't think you'd ever want to go under again—not that deep," Mr. Williams said grimly. "I didn't know there were big sharks out there, or I'd never have suggested trying to recover my watch!"

"They don't usually attack," Tony said mechanically.

The watch . . . that was the worst of it, he thought sadly. All this had been for nothing. He distinctly remembered that he'd still had the watch in his left hand when he drew his knife to stab the shark. Even after that. But when they hauled him into the launch, half conscious, he was empty-handed. Sometime during his agonizing fight for breath, in those last minutes after the air in his tank ran out, the watch must have slipped from his fingers and gone down again to the bottom of the bay.

"You can get another diver to find it," Tony said despondently. "We know it's there."

Mr. Williams shuddered. "Let it stay there! I'd never ask anyone to go down in the ocean again. And I want to pay you something, Tony, even though your mission wasn't successful."

"You already paid for the recompression chamber and the doctor," Tony muttered.

"But not for risking your life." Mr. Williams put three fifty-peso notes into Tony's hand. "It's little enough, my boy."

Tony looked at the money uncertainly. "I didn't really earn it. It was my own fault everything went wrong."

"You earned it," Mr. Williams assured him. "I've got to go back to the hotel now. We're checking out early in the morning. I hope you won't have any lasting ill effects from this, Tony. Good-by—and thank you for trying."

"I thank you, sir, for the money and for your kindness."

Left alone on the street, in front of the station, Tony and Peter looked at each other.

"Well, at least you got *something* out of it," Peter sighed. "I think he should have paid you the whole two hundred and fifty for almost getting drowned—or eaten by a shark! Are you sure you feel all right, Tony? Don't you want me to call a taxi to take you home?"

"Naw, I'm all right." Tony's voice was gruff. He was trying to think. First, he had been forbidden beach jobs, because of the fight. Now he was forbidden to dive, for another reason. It looked as though his chances were narrowing fast.

Peter knew what was on his friend's mind. "You can earn it some other way, Tony," he encouraged.

"Fishing," Tony said resolutely. "Night fishing. It's slow money but I'll get it, somehow. I have to get it! I'll see Don Clemente tomorrow. If his nephew is still going out with him, I'll try to team up with someone else."

"Do you think they'd take me, too?" Peter's voice was eager.

Tony smiled for the first time since his almost disastrous experience under water.

"I don't even know if they'll take me! Give me time to work this out, Pedro. And by the way, don't tell anyone about this accident this afternoon, will you? I just hope Uncle Juan doesn't hear about it."

"You know I never talk about your business," Peter said reproachfully.

"That's right, you don't." Tony squeezed Peter's shoulder. "You're a good friend, Pedro."

The next evening at sundown, Tony went around to the fishermen's beach. Don Clemente wasn't there yet, and Tony sat down on one of the overturned dugouts, looking around him.

Everything else in Acapulco was changing fast, he thought, but this little crescent-shaped strip of sand looked the same as it had looked for years: the native *canoas* pulled out under the trees, some upended and some covered with broad palm leaves to protect them from the strong sun during the day.

Youngsters were wading and swimming in the shallow water near the shore. Mexican buzzards, already overfed, picked without much interest at the fish heads strewn along the beach. A few boys and older men were dragging their dugouts to the water's edge, on wooden rollers. They worked easily, joking among themselves, their voices carrying in the early evening air. Tony watched them enviously, thinking how carefree they seemed to be.

When a stocky old man came down the beach, carrying round-bladed paddles over his shoulder, Tony got up.

"*Buenas noches,* Don Clemente."

"*Hola,* Tony. How are you?"

"I am all right, Don Clemente. I came to ask—is your nephew going with you tonight?"

The weather-beaten old face turned toward him, eyes sharp but kindly. "I doubt it, Tony. He hasn't shown up yet. Anyway, I guess he'd be glad to get out of it, if you want to come. He'd rather take his girl out. He's going to get married soon."

"Shall I run to his house and tell him that I'll take his place?"

"Oh, I'll just leave word with someone here, in case he comes," the old man said easily. "I hardly expect him now. I was going to look for another partner for tonight, anyway."

Grateful for this bit of luck, Tony eagerly helped in righting the heavy canoe. Wedging one of the short log rollers under the front and one under the back, they pushed the dugout toward the water. "*Ahora!*" Tug . . . rest . . . tug . . . rest . . . to where the water lapped the sand.

Don Clemente stowed away the night's provisions: lines, bait, a string bag containing a bottle of fresh water and a few tortillas.

Tony fitted forked sticks into the holes on either side of the *canoa* and hung the two gasoline lanterns on them.

He rolled his pants above his knees for the launching. There was an intent, almost devoted expression on his face that Don Clemente noticed as he straightened up.

"You like to fish, don't you, Tony?"

"More than anything—except diving."

"Not so many of the young people do, nowadays," Don Clemente sighed. "Too quiet for them, I suppose. Acapulco is full of excitement now—excitement and entertainment. Young folks are always on the go."

"I'm not—not the way you mean. I guess I'm the quiet type," Tony said.

"Well, we're ready, eh? Let's shove off."

They waited for a wave. "*Ahora!*" A big tug, with the water to help. They waited again. "Now!" Another tug and the boat was almost floating free.

"You get in, Don Clemente. I'll push off, the next one."

The old man swung into the boat with a single, practiced movement. With the next wave, Tony gave a strong push and jumped in the back. They settled down to paddling with the round-bladed paddles.

Thus began a series of night fishing trips which reminded Tony of the early years, when he had gone with his father to fish, and which would have been purest joy now, if the worry of financial success had not been ever-present.

But even with the gnawing specter of money always before him, those nights held hours of such vast peace and contentment that Tony could not bear to lose a moment of them in sleep, as Don Clemente sometimes did, dozing with the line tied loosely to his hand.

Out there on the ocean at night, the silence was immense, with only the gentle lapping of water as the long swells lifted the native *canoa*. The darkness was immense, too, beyond the glow of their lanterns. Sometimes phosphorescence made the water gleam like liquid silver. Every drop from the paddles sparkled and the fish glowed in magical gold or flowing green.

I could be happy with this—just this, Tony thought, if Uncle Juan would let me be. He liked to feel the pull on his line as they landed the shining red snappers, the black tunas, the corvinas, and many other kinds of fish. He liked the excitement of spearing the needlefish which sometimes leaped toward the light.

He liked to hear the occasional snatches of song that came over the water from other boats, and to see their lights, twinkling like fireflies around the bay.

He loved the cold dampness of the air and the hush of the pearl-colored dawns as they paddled back, with the sea turning pale blue-silver, the sky faintly tinged from the hidden sunrise.

He liked everything about it. He didn't even mind peddling the fish directly to the hard-faced buyers in the big tourist hotels, haggling to get a better price for it.

For the first few nights, the fishing was good and Tony's savings grew perceptibly. Twice they caught the prized dorado, weighing around fifty pounds each and bringing excellent prices. Tony began to think that the night fishing might be the answer to his problems, after all.

Once when Don Clemente seemed to be in a talkative mood, Tony questioned him.

"You've always lived in Acapulco, haven't you, Don Clemente?"

The old man nodded. "Born here. I've never been out of it, except three trips to Mexico City."

"And you've always fished for a living?"

"Always. Your father and I were partners for almost two years—before you were born."

"My uncle," Tony said slowly, "thinks no one can make a living by fishing, now. He says too many things can happen. Bad weather. Bad luck. He's convinced that a fixed salary is the only way to get ahead."

"Well, in a way he's right, Tony. Things have changed, you know. The cost of living has gone way up. It's much harder to live by fishing than it used to be. But I'm an old man. Too old to change now. I require very little, to live. My children are all married and living in other parts of the country. My nephew is planning to get a job in the capital, too. For a young man who will some day marry and have a family to support, this kind of fishing is no longer practical."

"But eventually I would have a fishing cruiser—to take tourists out, or to fish commercially along the coast."

"That is a different matter, of course. But launches are very expensive, and the cost of upkeep is tremendous."

"You and I have been doing all right with this, lately," Tony remarked.

"We've been—lucky," Don Clemente said cautiously, crossing himself. "It's better not to talk about it." After a moment he added, "Also, you're a good salesman, Tony!"

Tony smiled a little at the old man's combination of superstition and religion and business.

But he didn't smile a few days later, when they returned to the beach in the morning with only a few small fish to show for their long night's work. And the night following that was even worse.

Don Clemente shrugged. "The current has changed. The water's too warm, now. The fish stay too far out— and too deep. That's the way it goes, my boy."

Tony refused to give up and the two continued their nightly excursions, although most of the other dugouts now remained on the beach at night, their owners accepting the inevitable.

On Christmas Eve, Tony again invited Peter and Mr. Carson to a neighborhood celebration, and they accepted the invitation with alacrity.

The fiesta was much the same as the first *posada* they had attended, except that this time the cradle in the manger was no longer empty. A doll representing the Christ Child had been placed there, and the guests sang it to sleep with the gentle lullaby which all Mexican mothers sing to their children.

At midnight, the church bells began to ring and a hiss of fireworks exploded from the plaza. Showers of bright stars rained over the town, heralding Christmas Day.

Tony enjoyed the fiesta, but he was anxious to get back to work. Even on Christmas night, he and Don Clemente continued the fishing, unprofitable though it was. Tony also worked many days, fishing with Peter off the rocks in the coves and inlets.

Don Clemente had allowed the American boy to go with them twice, at night, although three persons were really too many for the small dugout. Peter did not talk

much, during the fishing, any more than Don Clemente
did. But a current of kindred feeling ran between the
two boys.

It was strange, Tony mused, that the person he felt
closest to, now, was an American boy he hadn't even
known four months ago.

When the fishing was bad, Tony sometimes sang during the long nights, to keep from worrying too much.
And one night, a few days after Christmas, he urged Don
Clemente to tell him about the old days in Acapulco, to
pass the time.

"I wish I could have seen the town the way it was
when you were a boy," he said wistfully.

"It was different, all right," the old man said. "So
different that sometimes I can hardly believe it's the
same place."

"Tell me about it," Tony begged.

"Well, it was a sleepy little village, with no tourists,
no hotels to speak of, few roads—and those unpaved."

He paused while Tony suddenly jerked his line and
pulled it in. A piece of seaweed was clinging to it, and
Tony silently detached the weed, rebaited his hook and
let it out again.

"Caleta Beach, for example," Don Clemente went on.
"Now it's famous all over the world, and it's only five
minutes from the center of town, on a wide, beautiful
boulevard. When I was young, it was almost inaccessible! Out in the country! It was a real occasion when we
went there for an all-day picnic. It took hours to go
around the peninsula in rowboats. Or if we went by land,
there was a difficult, narrow path—"

His voice died abruptly. Tony, who was looking at the water, thought that the old man was silently reminiscing. But finally the silence became so prolonged that he decided Don Clemente had fallen asleep right while he was talking. He turned to glance at him—and saw that the old fisherman had slumped down, his knees in the bilge water at the bottom of the boat, his back resting awkwardly against the board seat. His face had sagged and the glazed eyes were half open.

"Don Clemente!" Tony's voice was loud with alarm. Swinging around in his seat, he crawled toward the old man, taking care not to tilt the clumsy dugout. "Don Clemente! What's the matter?"

The old man made a gurgling sound in his throat, and he seemed to be trying to focus his eyes on the boy.

Tony stared at him, frightened. Was the man dying? Was it a heart attack? He scanned the water, looking for other boats. But few fishermen had come out this night, and he could see only one light, far away toward the open sea.

There was only one thing to do—get back to Acapulco as soon as possible. Scarcely daring to touch the old man, for fear of making his condition worse, Tony took off his own jacket and cushioned Don Clemente's head, as best he could, against the stern. Then he started paddling rapidly back toward the coast.

It seemed an interminable distance, with only one person paddling, and with worry his only companion. The first faint light of day was beginning to show in the sky when Tony finally pulled up to the beach and called for help.

One man ran to a telephone, while others crowded around the *canoa,* offering suggestions. In a very few minutes, an ambulance came screaming along the boulevard, and the old man was lifted onto a stretcher and taken to the hospital. Tony went with him.

"It's a light stroke," the doctor said, after he had made his examination. "He may be all right in a few weeks—and he may not. Do you know where to get in touch with his family, boy?"

"They've all moved away from Acapulco. That's all he told me," Tony answered. "Even his nephew who used to fish with him left last week. But I'll find out from his neighbors."

For the next two days, Tony hardly moved from Don Clemente's side, except to visit the neighbors and to send telegrams to relatives. On the afternoon of New Year's Eve, Don Clemente's son arrived from Mexico City, to take over, and by that time the old man was improving. Although he still could not speak intelligibly, his eyes thanked Tony for all he had done.

"He's going to get better," the doctor said confidently. "These old fishermen are tough! He'll live a long time yet."

A shadow of a grin touched Don Clemente's lips and he nodded slightly. Tony squeezed the old man's inert hand.

"I'm glad," he said simply. "I'll leave you with your son now, Don Clemente. But I'll come back to see you, often."

Peter was waiting for him on the street in front of the

hospital, and the two boys started walking slowly toward town.

"Well, that's that," Tony sighed. "That's the end of the night fishing."

"Maybe we could borrow his boat while he's sick," Peter said tentatively. "I could be your partner."

Tony shook his head. "You can't fish nights and go to school days, Pedro," he said, not mentioning that Peter's lack of experience would be a handicap rather than a help. "Besides," he added soberly, "there haven't been enough fish, this last week, to bother with paddling out there. It would average out enough to live on, all year round, but not enough to save the money *I* need, quickly."

Peter didn't answer. Glancing at him, Tony saw that he was looking at a dark-faced boy who was crossing the street ahead of them.

11

Chico's Plan

"THAT'S THE BOY WHO BROUGHT US BACK FROM THE ISLAND, the first time you took me skin diving," Peter remarked. "What was his name—Chico?"

Tony nodded, his face thoughtful. "Aunt Raquel says he's been around to the house twice, looking for me. I think he has some kind of business scheme in his head."

"Maybe it's something that would help you out during the next month," Peter suggested.

Tony stood hesitating. "I don't know why I don't really trust Chico any more," he muttered. "I've known him a long time. We were in school together. But lately . . ." His voice trailed off.

Well, it was almost like an omen, he thought. He had been reluctant to seek Chico out, but now he had run right into him. He quickened his steps a little, and the dark-faced boy wheeled around.

"Tony! I've been looking all over for you! Where you been keeping yourself?"

"I've been busy," Tony answered. "Fishing day and night."

"I want to see you—alone." Chico's eyes flicked over

Peter. "I have something *very* important to tell you."

"You can talk in front of Pedro." Tony put his hand on the blond boy's shoulder. "He is my *cuate*—my twin. I have no secrets from him."

"But this has to be no more than two people," Chico insisted.

Tony shrugged, feeling almost relieved. "If it's that secret, you better not tell me, either," he said, preparing to walk away.

"Tony—wait!" Chico's voice was urgent. "All right, let him come. But we can't talk here." He looked around cautiously. "Come across the street to the café. I'll buy you a *refresco*."

When the three boys were seated around a table in the middle of the restaurant—deserted at that hour of the afternoon—and Chico was satisfied that they were quite alone, he leaned forward, his sun-blackened gamin face tense with excitement.

"First of all, you must promise me one thing. Whether or not you go in with me on this, you will not say anything to anyone about it—ever!"

"You know I don't talk," Tony said dryly. "Pedro doesn't, either. Go on."

"Well, you remember what I said that day in the launch—about getting rich quick?"

"Yes, I've been thinking about it lately," Tony admitted. "You said something about guiding tourists, since I speak English."

Chico's face was smug. "You can't work with tourists now. That fight with Lencho—that was a bad thing, *hombre!* And now you can't dive, either."

Tony was not surprised that Chico knew all about it. The grapevine around the docks operated with amazing efficiency.

"Never mind that," Tony said brusquely. "So what do you have in mind?"

Chico sipped his orangeade, obviously enjoying the suspense.

"This is something so big, Tony—you'll be able to buy the biggest fishing cruiser on the bay, if you want to. And I'll buy a car—a brand-new Chevrolet—"

Tony's lips were setting with exasperation and after another stealthy look around to be certain there was no one within earshot, Chico hurried on, "You remember old Adan, in Puerto Marques?"

"Of course." Tony nodded, showing his surprise. What could old Adan have to do with money? When they were young boys, Tony and Chico had often visited the grizzled old man when they went to dive and swim in Puerto Marques, a small and beautiful bay around a curve in the coast from Acapulco.

The old man lived alone on his small coconut grove and liked to have the boys come. He gave them coconuts and regaled them with bloodcurdling and partly true stories, handed down for generations, of the days when pirates had hidden out in Puerto Marques, waiting for the prize of the Pacific traffic: the Manila ship which plied between the Philippines and Spain by way of Acapulco, carrying rich cargo from the Orient.

"What about Adan?" Tony asked curiously.

"He died about two weeks ago," Chico answered impressively. "And before he died, he sent for me. To give me something!"

"A map showing where there's buried treasure, I suppose?" Tony scoffed. "Chico, I thought you had better sense!"

The boys of Acapulco were brought up on stories of buried treasure. All of them went through a period of dreaming, or even of actually digging, to find the pirate chests that were said to be hidden in the surrounding hills. But nothing was ever discovered. Perhaps because there was much superstition attached to the tales of treasure. It was said that ghosts guarded the buried loot and a curse fell on those who tried to take it away from them.

"Tony, you're not superstitious!" Chico challenged.

"No. I just think that if there was anything around here, somebody got it long ago."

"This is different," Chico said with convincing confidence. "You know Adan and his father and his grandfather have all lived on that coconut grove. But they also owned land beyond that—back in the swamp. It's all overgrown with brush now. But there *is* a map and besides, Adan told me how to find the hidden treasure!"

"If they knew it was there, why didn't Adan or his father dig it up?" Tony asked skeptically. "They were poor."

"You know how they feel about it over there," Chico said. "They're afraid of that curse. Adan's father wouldn't go near the place. Adan himself—" Chico paused to let his words sink in. "Adan himself, when he was younger, dug until he found it—and then covered it up again! That's how he knows it's there."

Tony and Peter both stared incredulously and Peter spoke this time, his voice trembling with excitement, "You mean to say he actually saw treasure and then buried it again! That's crazy!"

"He swears that's what he did," Chico said seriously. "He found a chest and opened it enough to see that it had gold and precious stones. And then, he said, suddenly the sky was full of lightning and there was a roar of thunder—though this was in the dry season, mind you! He covered it up and never went back. He said he didn't want gold at the cost of his life."

"Then why did he give the map to you—to let *you* get killed?" Tony jeered. "I thought he was your friend!"

"He didn't think the ghost was there any more." Chico seemed unmoved by Tony's skepticism. "He had a dream some months ago, saying it was time to dig up the treasure. He was an old man then and knew he hadn't long to live. He didn't care about the money any more—"

"Didn't he have any relatives?" Peter broke in.

Chico frowned at the interruption. "No," he said shortly. "There was a younger brother who moved somewhere up north when he was still a young man, but he died many years ago. The brother's only son—Adan's nephew, of course—wrote to his uncle for a while after his father's death, but then he stopped writing and Adan heard later that he'd been killed in an accident."

"Well, go on," Tony said impatiently, as Chico paused.

"Adan didn't care about the money for himself," Chico

repeated, "but he felt that it was wrong not to tell someone about it. So he called me and gave me the map. He
died the next morning."

Tony was silent, thinking it over. The story was fantastic. He didn't believe any of that about the thunder
and lightning and the dreams. But about the treasure—
there was a bare possibility. Suppose—just suppose—that
one of the few remaining pirate caches *was* on old Adan's
property! It was not impossible. Chico was pretty shrewd
and he obviously believed that he was onto something
authentic.

A wave of excitement prickled Tony's scalp. He
glanced at Peter. The American boy's face was entranced. Even Peter was beginning to believe.

Tony sat lost in thought. He was excited but he was
also uneasy. Treasure hunting for the fun of it was one
thing, but this was something else. He didn't quite like
the furtiveness and greed he saw in Chico's face.

Two months ago, he would probably have refused to
have anything to do with the project. He had never
wanted money in itself. But Uncle Juan had forced the
need for quick money on him by setting an impossible
goal. And impossible goals required impossible—or im-
probable—means of achieving them. This was a slim
chance but if it *did* work . . .

Tony let himself dream, for a moment, of what it
would mean to him: money to buy a boat, skin-diving
equipment, everything he needed to earn a living doing
the things he liked to do and was best fitted to do. It
would mean release from his obligation to Uncle Juan

and the threat of living in the city. It would mean money to help Marta through school.

Chico's voice cut through his thoughts. "Well? Make up your mind, Tony! What's the matter? Are you afraid?"

Tony smiled a little. "No," he said calmly. "I don't believe in ghosts and I'm not afraid of them. Sure, I'll go in with you. When do we start?"

"I thought we should wait till after New Year's, when there'll be fewer fiestas and fewer people around to see us." Chico's voice was eager again. "What about day after tomorrow—Wednesday?"

Tony nodded agreement.

"We should get there about sundown," Chico went on. "We'll need a machete, a lantern, a pickax and two shovels. And we mustn't be seen coming in with them. Our only real danger is from the Puerto Marques natives. You know how they are about outsiders. If they think we're coming to take anything away from their land, they're capable of killing us."

Peter's blue eyes grew round with incredulity, but Tony knew that what Chico said was true. The people of Puerto Marques were very jealous of their small bay village and of its traditions. Outsiders who overstepped their rights were ruthlessly dealt with. Although Tony and Chico had spent enough time there so that their mere presence would arouse no suspicion, nevertheless even they would not be allowed to go around unmolested if they were armed with machetes and shovels.

"I can get the machete and a lantern," Tony said, "if you can get the other stuff."

Chico nodded. "I'll get them. And I think I can borrow the launch I'm working on now. We'll have to buy the gasoline, of course. I believe we should take our skin-diving masks. That way it will look more natural. We'll leave about three o'clock and really do some skin diving till nearly dark. Then we can hide the boat in one of the coves, take the tools and go to the site."

Tony looked at him. "You seem to have everything all worked out."

Chico grinned. "Well, I haven't been thinking of anything else for the last week!"

The waiter came with the check as the boys were completing their plans. It was dusk by now and Tony suddenly jumped up.

"I've been so far away," he said ruefully, "for a minute I almost forgot it's New Year's Eve. We're having a small fiesta at the house tonight and they'll be wondering where I am. Do you want to come, Chico? Pedro is coming."

Chico shook his head. "It will be better if we don't see each other until Wednesday. I'll be around, early that morning, to check with you."

"Okay."

The three boys left the restaurant and stood for a moment on the street, excitement and conspiracy binding them together, making them reluctant to part.

Then Chico broke the spell by saying rudely, "You're not going with us Wednesday, gringo. Three is too many —attracts too much attention."

"He is not going with us," Tony said quietly, "but for another reason."

"Tony!" Peter's voice was stunned with disappointment.

Chico interrupted, satisfied that things were going his way, "Well, I'm off now, Tony. See you Wednesday."

Tony nodded and watched the short boy disappearing into the darkness.

"I guess I won't go to the fiesta, after all." Peter's voice was more hurt and angry than Tony had ever heard it. "We aren't such close friends as I thought. You don't trust me!"

"Pedro, you know how I feel about you." Tony put his hand on one of the thin shoulders. "You are my brother. You are the best friend I ever had. But this could be dangerous—maybe *very* dangerous. I got you in trouble before. I don't want to do it again. Your father trusts me."

"If my father gives permission, will you take me?" Peter's voice was tense.

Tony hesitated. "Your father is like you are, Pedro—too kindhearted and confiding to know what some of our people can be like when they're aroused. He might let you go, not realizing the danger."

"Probably the most exciting adventure I'd ever have in my life!" Peter said bitterly. "You *have* to let me go, Tony! I'll never forgive you if you don't."

Tony sighed, remembering the way Peter had been working to help him.

"All right," he said slowly, "but if anything bad happens to you, *amigo*, I'm the one who would never forgive myself!"

Peter pounded Tony's back in happy relief. "Nothing

will happen," he said. "We either find the treasure or we don't, that's all. I'll go home now, Tony, and put on a clean shirt for the party. See you later!"

In spite of the fact that he was late, Tony did not go home immediately. He walked across to the docks and stood looking at the still, dark mirror of the bay. Chills of excitement kept running through him. Common sense told him not to hope; yet he could not help hoping.

At the same time, he was filled with uneasiness. Uncle Juan would not approve of this method of getting money, if he knew of it. Tony didn't really approve of it himself. But if money was so important, what difference did it make how he got it, so long as he didn't steal it or hurt anyone else in getting it?

As he turned to go home, his feeling of apprehension was suddenly increased as he saw a familiar figure watching him from across the boulevard. Lencho was standing in front of the restaurant where the boys had laid their plans!

As Tony stood staring, the figure disappeared quickly around the corner of the building onto another street.

What was Lencho doing there, watching him? Could he have heard anything about the treasure hunting? The boys had been seated in the middle of an empty restaurant and had kept their voices low. No, probably Lencho had just happened along now and had noticed Tony on the docks. There was no doubt that he was waiting for an opportune moment to finish the fight that had started on the beach, but Tony wasn't too worried about that. He felt he could take care of himself.

Just the same, it was an odd coincidence that his glass-bottomed boat enemy should be standing right there, in that particular spot. . . .

As Tony started up the slope toward home, he could hear the New Year's Eve firecrackers popping already, and he smelled the pungent odor of the smoke. This would go on, increasing in volume, until at midnight the deafening clamor of rockets, church bells, boat whistles and pistol shots ushered in the new year.

What would the new year hold for him? Tony wondered. Perhaps this treasure-hunting expedition would make all the difference! This was his last chance for big money. It *had* to work out!

12

Hunting for Treasure

THE RED BALL OF SUN WAS SINKING FAST TOWARD THE faint horizon line that separated violet sea from sky. It made a gold path between the two low mountain ranges that embraced the Bay of Puerto Marques.

Tony took a quick look at the sky as Chico surfaced from a dive beside the launch where he and Peter were sitting.

"I think that's enough diving," he said in a low voice. "Surely everyone on the beach has seen us here now, innocently whiling away an afternoon. Besides, they'll know it's too dark to skin dive now, anyhow. Let's go over toward Mayahua Cove and throw out a fishing line. Then, as soon as it gets a little darker, we'll ease the launch around the point and hide it. Everyone will think we've gone back to Acapulco."

Chico grunted and climbed into the launch without answering. He was in an ugly mood. He'd been surly ever since Tony had insisted that Peter go with them. He seemed to think that three boys would attract ten times as much attention as two. But Tony had refused to go without his American friend and Chico had had to give in, ungraciously.

Chico was nervous, Tony could see. Well, he was a little nervous himself but he didn't intend to show it! He glanced at Peter. He didn't believe his gringo friend was nervous but he certainly was excited!

Ever since Chico had shown them the parchment map that old Adan had given him, Peter had hardly been able to contain himself. Tony knew how he felt. There weren't many boys who had a chance to hunt for treasure, these days, guided by a parchment map. Not even in Acapulco!

From the moment they had seen the map, with its queer drawings of the lagoon and the trees and the faded, ancient-looking, wrongly spelled labelings in Spanish, the whole project had begun to seem more real to both Tony and Peter. Tony had begun to hope. Before that, he had entered into the scheme simply because there *might* be a chance, and he had nothing to lose and everything to gain.

Now he found himself actually counting on it, in spite of all the warnings of his cautious nature.

The three of them were sitting in silence as the launch chugged slowly toward Mayahua Cove. Tony finally spoke, to lighten the tension.

"When we stop outside the cove, let's have another look at that map, Chico," he suggested. "Before the daylight goes. Afterward it'll be too dark to see it well, even with a lantern."

Chico nodded grudgingly and kept his eyes on the water ahead. Tony winked at Peter and shrugged his shoulders, indicating in pantomime that there was nothing to be done about Chico's bad humor but that he, Tony, was glad to have his friend along.

Peter closed one of his blue eyes in an answering wink. They understood each other perfectly.

"The sun's gone," Peter said after a moment, in a low voice. "I've thought, these last three days, that this moment would never come!"

Tony grinned a little. "But we have to pretend to fish for a while," he warned. "All these precautions probably seem foolish to you, Pedro. But you don't know these people over here. They don't want *anyone* treasure hunting in their village, or anywhere near it! And they can get very nasty about it."

"Why don't you say it right out," Chico put in impatiently. "They usually murder people they find digging."

"I don't care much for that word." Tony kept his voice calm. "Throw the line over—and then let's have a look at that map."

Chico cast an anxious eye toward the beach, but it was practically deserted now, in the gathering dusk. A few people who owned refreshment stands were cleaning up after the day's business. No one seemed at all interested in the launch out by the cove. Chico took the slender cylinder of parchment from a cloth bag and unrolled it carefully. The three boys bent over it.

"This is approximately where we are now," Tony said, indicating a spot on the map. "We can beach the boat on a little strip of sand around this point here. There's a trail that goes part way up Diamond Mountain and then forks, with one path going on back to the lagoon behind the village."

"I know," Chico broke in impatiently. "I've been on that path. It will bring us out about here." He pointed to a spot on the thin parchment. "Then we'll have about half a kilometer to walk along the lagoon, to where the two amate trees are. Near those two trees there are directions on a rock. Old Adan told me how to decipher them."

"Okay," Tony said, his voice shaking a little. "Put the map away. I guess we don't need it any more."

They sat for a few minutes in silence, waiting for deeper dark, each boy so occupied with his own thoughts that they all jumped when Chico felt a pull on his line and began to draw it in.

"Throw it back," Tony said in a low voice. "This is once we don't want to bother with fish."

At last, satisfied that they could no longer be seen from the shore, Tony and Chico paddled softly around the point, not daring to use the motor now. In a few minutes they had pulled the boat high on a tiny, hidden beach and were gathering together the equipment they had brought.

"We can't use the lantern until we reach the rock," Chico said. "It's dangerous enough, even then."

"I brought along a little pencil flashlight of my father's," Peter whispered, even the whisper betraying his excitement. "If I shield it with my hand, they can't see it from shore, and it will give us a little light, anyway."

"Didn't I tell you three heads were better than two?" Tony reminded Chico. "That was a good idea, Pedro!"

Chico said nothing.

"You know the path," Tony said. "You go first with the machete and lantern, then Pedro with the flashlight and the pickax. I'll come last with the shovels."

In that order they started up the trail, single file. There was little brush to clear away here and they made good time until they reached the fork. One path, fairly open, went on up over the mountain. The other one, leading back down to the lagoon, was not much used, and now the boys had to stop every few minutes while Chico hacked away at the lush foliage that grew in thick tangles over the hillside and down to the water, even dipping into the sea. There were giant ferns, creeping lianas, and there was a strong odor of night-blooming jasmine, along with the more rank odors of tropical jungle.

The breeze had dropped at sunset and even here, on an elevation above the water, the night was suddenly sultry. Tony could feel the perspiration trickling down under his open shirt and he knew that Chico, wielding the machete up ahead, must be even warmer. He pushed past Peter.

"I'll take my turn with the machete," he whispered to Chico. "I know the path well enough."

"I'll do it," Chico answered shortly. "You keep a watch behind us."

It was impossible to watch much, Tony thought, when you couldn't see your hand in front of your face. Peter was keeping the tiny light of his flashlight trained ahead, to help Chico.

Tony dropped back again, putting his hand on Peter's shoulder. "How does it go, *amigo?* Not frightened?"

"No," Peter breathed. "I'm so glad you brought me, Tony!"

"Don't talk!" Chico hissed, although his machete was inevitably making more noise than the boys' hushed voices.

A few minutes later, Chico stopped so abruptly that Peter ran into him. "Did you feel a *temblor?*" he asked in a shaky voice.

Tony couldn't resist teasing him. "You think we're going to have an earthquake for our treasure hunting, instead of thunder and lightning in the dry season?" he asked mildly.

Chico went on without answering.

Tony had felt the earth tremble slightly but it didn't bother him. Light tremors were common in Acapulco. What *did* bother him was a feeling he had had for several minutes that they were being followed.

Imagination! he scoffed at himself. The whole setup invited your mind to play tricks on you.

But a moment later the feeling came again, more strongly. He put his hand ahead to touch Peter's arm, and then found Chico's.

"Wait," he said, in a voice so soft that it might have been the sighing of the trees. "Wait a minute and put out your light, Pedro."

The three boys stood motionless in the darkness. A twig snapped somewhere, far back, and then the silence was complete except for the faint sound of a brook gurgling in the distance, the patter of night things moving through the jungle, the whir of insects.

"What was it?" Chico whispered.

"Nothing, I guess."

Tony strained his ears. He could not hear the following steps now, but he had the impression that they had stopped, too, when that twig snapped. He had a strong feeling that there was something behind them on the path—some distance behind. It might be only a small animal—but would an animal be as stealthy as that?

However, there was no stopping now. If someone was behind them, they were cut off from the boat. By going on, they could, if they had to, fling their tools in the brush, cut over toward the village and hope to look as though they had been on an innocent hike.

"Let's hurry," he said, as calmly as he could. "Never mind the lianas, Chico. We'll duck them. Don't do any more chopping than you have to."

They went on more quickly, pushing through the jungle growth which seemed to reach out long fingers and grab at them in the darkness, scratching their faces and arms. Perspiration was streaming from them and the insects were a constant irritation.

"It can't be far now," Tony panted.

Physical discomfort had almost made him forget his sensation that they were being followed. Then, during a pause when they stopped for breath, he heard it again: barely distinguishable, furtive sounds on the path behind them.

"I think we're being followed," he whispered to the other two boys. "Let's run for it. Once we get to the lagoon, perhaps we can lose them."

Ten minutes later they arrived, breathless, at the edge of the swamp, among the mangrove trees. They stopped

and listened. There was no sound now, except the occasional trickling of water over the great roots of the
trees, and the wild singing of mosquitoes. The heat here
was suffocating, like a physical thing bearing down on
them.

As they hesitated, they could feel another faint trembling of the earth beneath them. Chico stiffened.

"Man, I've never felt it so hot in my entire life!" he
muttered. "And so still! Not a breath of air. Let's get this
over with! Half a kilometer to the right, now—"

It was on the tip of Tony's tongue to taunt Chico with
being scared, but he thought better of it and turned to
Peter instead.

"How you doing, Pedro?" he whispered.

"Okay!" Peter's voice was shaking with excitement but
there was no fear in it, and Tony was proud of his
friend's courage.

They started off on a faint trail that followed the winding of the lagoon. But it was rough going. The big trees
closed like a ceiling above them, blotting out the friendly
sky and stars. The twisting roots of the mangroves made
a hopeless tangle under their feet. All of them stumbled
constantly, and once Chico went sprawling into the slimy
lagoon and came up gasping and furious, covered with
evil-smelling mud.

"*Caramba,*" he spluttered. "If I had known it was like
this—"

The half kilometer seemed interminable. Strange
vapors rose from the surface of the swamp. From time to
time they could see gleaming pairs of small fiery eyes—
belonging to what creatures?

Tony told himself that he wasn't afraid. But this place was certainly a lot different at night than it was by day! He took off his shirt, mopped his streaming face and chest, and then put it on again as protection against the insects.

Chico had taken Peter's pencil flashlight and was vainly searching for the two amate trees which were the signposts to the hidden treasure.

"We must have missed them," he muttered savagely. "Seems to me we've come at least four kilometers."

"Well, we haven't," Tony contradicted. "It just seems that way because the walking's so hard. They must be right along here somewhere."

They stumbled around in the tangled growth for another half hour. Tony sensed that Chico was about ready to give up the whole expedition. But he himself didn't intend to back out now, not after they had come this far!

"Stay here a minute and rest," he whispered to Chico and Peter, taking the flashlight from Chico's hand. "Let me see if I can find them."

For once, Chico was in agreement. Without a word, he sat down wearily on a mangrove root and leaned back against the tree.

"I'm going with you," Peter murmured.

Tony started to object, but then he took his friend's hand and the two of them carefully explored the surroundings. Within five minutes, Tony had located the amate trees and shortly afterward they found a slab of rock with strange markings on it.

"This must be it!" he said jubilantly.

They went back for Chico, whose short rest seemed to have revived him. And a few minutes later, after lighting the lantern, they were deciding on the exact spot to dig.

While they were clearing the place of underbrush with the machete they heard a strange sound, like a distant rumble.

"*What was that?*" Chico's voice was terrified. He stood paralyzed, the machete motionless in his raised hand. Even Tony felt the hair rise on the back of his neck.

They stood listening for several minutes. It was eerie! The rumbling beneath them . . . the lantern light elongating the shadows and making the surroundings beyond the circle of illumination seem even blacker. . . .

"Come on," Peter said finally. "Let's dig."

Chico neither moved nor spoke for another minute, but finally he began working again, with some reluctance.

They had cleared the ground and had removed the first few shovelfuls of soft earth when suddenly, without warning, several figures jumped on them from behind. Chico let out a wild scream, and Tony's heart bounced crazily.

It was soon evident that these were no supernatural spirits. They weren't Puerto Marques natives, either, guarding their village from treasure seekers. Tony, struggling furiously with whoever—or whatever—had pinioned his arms from behind, immediately recognized an ugly voice that said, "Let me at him! Tony's mine!"

So it was Lencho and his pals who had been following them!

Somehow his old enemy had found out where they

were going and had followed, probably with a double purpose: to even his score with Tony and to latch onto the treasure for himself. To ensure success, he had brought enough reinforcements to outnumber the three boys.

Tony's lips curled in contempt for Lencho's cowardice, even as he felt a smashing blow to his cheek. Jerking one arm loose with a quick, ducking movement, he lashed out blindly in front of him, but he missed. It was impossible to see anything. The lantern had been knocked over in the scuffle and had gone out, though he could hear Chico's babbling fury, exclamations of unknown voices and the continuous sound of blows.

Outnumbered and exhausted as they were, there was little doubt as to who would win this time, he thought in despair. He had really gotten Peter into trouble now!

Then, just as a sixth sense made him duck a fist that was aimed at his eye, everything seemed to break loose! There was a deep, menacing rumble such as they had heard before, but much louder now. And immediately the ground under their feet began to oscillate slowly.

"*Temblor!*" It was Lencho's voice, this time, that rose to a shrill shriek.

All the boys stood paralyzed for a moment, the fight temporarily forgotten, in the face of this ominous threat from nature. While they stood, it came again—the uncanny rumble and an even stronger jolt. In the distance they could hear dislodged rocks from the mountains splashing into the sea.

"It's a warning!" Lencho cried in panic. "I'm getting out of here!"

His henchmen evidently agreed. There was a sudden wild scramble through the brush, and then the dip of paddles.

So they had followed along the lagoon in a canoe, Tony thought, with one part of his brain. That was how they had made such good time.

But there was something more important on his mind than how they had come—and gone. "Pedro!" he called urgently. "Where are you? Are you all right?"

"I'm all right." For the first time since Tony had known him, Peter's voice was a little shaken and scared. "They just held me down. It was you Lencho was after."

"And me!" Chico's voice came out of the darkness, filled with abject fear. "But Lencho was right—this is a warning! No more digging for me! I'm going—just as soon as they get far enough away so they don't all jump me in the dark!"

"Well, I'm not," Tony said, so relieved nothing had happened to Peter that the rest of it seemed unimportant. "That was just a coincidence—that quake coming right then. It's got nothing to do with our digging. Since we're here, we're going to find that treasure, if there is any!"

Chico protested violently but in the end he stayed— probably because he was afraid to go back alone, Tony thought.

It was the mangrove roots that made the digging all but impossible, they discovered. The earth itself was soft, but the far-spreading, tough roots grew in a wild tangle, below the ground as well as above it. For the next hour, the three boys worked harder than they had ever worked in their lives, chopping frantically with machete and pickax until the blades were dulled, and then pulling at the roots with their bare hands. Perspiration ran from them in rivers.

"We'd have done better to bring a saw," Chico said finally, with deep disgust. He was still edgy and he stopped every few minutes to listen. But the earth seemed to have settled down to normal. Besides the usual jungle noises, there were no sounds other than those they were making.

They had gone down about five feet and even Tony was almost ready to give up when suddenly, as he swung the pick, it contacted something hard, with a ring of metal.

"We've struck something!"

Galvanized into new life, their weariness forgotten, the three boys began to dig like mad.

It was a frenzied half hour before they were able to uncover enough of a small corroded metal chest to dig the rusted cover off with the pickax.

His hands trembling with excitement, Tony picked up the lantern and held it over the now lidless iron box.

Grinning up at them was a skull!

There was nothing else in the box except a handful of small bones.

"I think," Tony said grimly, "that our friend Adan was a practical joker."

Just then, the earth shook again and some of the dirt they had removed dropped on the grinning skull.

For Chico, it was the last straw of the unnerving night. He fell back, choking, and began to gibber hysterically as he turned to run. Tony grabbed his arm and shook him roughly until the babbling subsided into half sobs.

"Don't be a fool," Tony said curtly. "Sit down over there and keep quiet, while Pedro and I cover this up. We can't leave it like this."

Chico, too unmanned to have a mind of his own, obeyed him. Tony and Peter pushed back the earth which they had excavated with such pains.

As he silently shoveled damp dirt into the hole, it seemed to Tony that he was covering up his last hope.

He tried to tell himself that he had known all along that there wouldn't be anything. But it wasn't true. Toward the end he had really believed. And the disappointment now was crushing.

"Tony, I'm sorry." They were the first words Peter had uttered since they found the skull, and his voice was uneven.

Tony nodded without speaking. He hardly knew whether it was sweat or tears that ran down his face as they pushed some brush over the filled-in excavation and then started wearily back along the cruel trail beside the lagoon.

THIS BOOK IS THE PROPERTY OF THE
Georgia State Board of Education
AND IS FURNISHED TO

Miller County Library

JAMES S. PETERS, Chairman
DR. CLAUDE PURCELL, State Supt. of Schools

13

Aboard the *Albacora*

"PEDRO, THE MORE I THINK ABOUT IT," TONY SAID SLOWLY, "the more absolutely certain I am that we didn't find just the right spot—or the right treasure chest."

It was three days after the disastrous treasure hunt and the two boys were sitting on the edge of the dock, with their legs hanging over. They had fishing lines in their hands but they were much more interested in their private counsel of war than they were in the small bait fish they were catching.

Peter looked at Tony rather anxiously. "You're not letting this thing get you, are you, Tony? I mean—" He hesitated. "It can get to be a kind of fever, you know, like hunting for gold mines. People get delusions—you know what I mean?"

Tony put his hand on Peter's shoulder in reassurance. "Yes, I know what you mean. I thought it was something like that with Chico, at first. It *can* get to be a kind of madness. But it isn't that, with me. I've been thinking hard about this whole thing, the last three days."

He pulled in a small fish and threw it on the dock. Peter waited, still looking doubtful.

"Did you feel that?" Tony asked suddenly. "Another tremor. They keep on and on!"

Acapulco had been shaken by several small quakes since the big one the night the boys were digging in Puerto Marques. Most of the tremors were very small, but they were driving some of the tourists away and were getting to be nerve-racking to the townspeople. Even Uncle Juan, always so cool and composed, had seemed jumpy and paler than usual, lately.

"Never mind the tremor," Peter said impatiently. "*What* have you been thinking these last three days?"

"That we were foolish to give up so easily. You see, Pedro, you didn't know Adan. I did. What I said that night—about his being a practical joker—was just because I was disappointed. He wasn't that kind of person at all. He was an honest, serious, kindly old man. He wouldn't have given that map to Chico unless he'd really thought there was treasure there. We've got to try again, Pedro! I have a feeling—a very strong feeling—that we'll find something the next time!"

"Well, I'm sure willing." Peter's eyes sparkled. "When do we go? Tonight?"

"No. We've got to wait." Tony sighed. "I haven't told you yet what I was doing yesterday—when you came to the house and I wasn't there."

"No, you were very secretive about it." Peter's voice was a little hurt.

"Well, I'll tell you now. I went to Puerto Marques by bus and looked up a boy I know. Armando, his name is. He used to live here in Acapulco and I knew him pretty well. He's the only person in Puerto Marques I can trust to really keep our secret. He told me they've set a round-the-clock guard on Adan's property. They must have found out we were there—though I was sure we'd covered that hole up too well for anybody to notice it."

Peter's face fell. "Then how are we going to do it?"

"They won't keep that up very long," Tony said confidently. "I know those people. They're lazy. If nothing happens for a few nights, they'll forget all about the guard."

"How are we going to know?"

"Armando's going to watch for us. When they take the guard off, he'll let us know. I've promised him a percentage of whatever we find."

"And Chico?"

Tony shrugged. "He was so scared the other night that he doesn't want anything more to do with it. He's still sick from the fright he got."

The two boys were silent for a few minutes, thinking.

Then Tony said, "I still feel kind of guilty about this whole deal, Pedro. I'm sure Uncle Juan wouldn't like it, if he knew about it. But there are only three weeks left before the family goes. I've *got* to get that money before then. I doubt if they'll watch that property even a week. We'll just have to take the chance—and wait."

Peter nodded. "I wish—" he began.

But Tony motioned him to silence. A heavy-set man had come up behind them. They looked up.

"You're Tony Castillo, aren't you?" the man asked.

"Yes, Captain Ruiz." Tony got to his feet. "At your service."

"I see you know me." The captain smiled.

"Everyone knows the captain of the *Albacora*, sir." Tony's admiring eyes found the big fishing cruiser which was moored a little distance away down the docks. "She's my favorite boat."

"Well, that's good. How would you like to be mate on her for a couple of weeks? My regular mate went on a business trip to Chilpancingo."

"I'd like it fine!" Tony's eyes were bright. "How did you—I mean, who—?"

"I happened to mention to Julio, on Caletilla Beach, that I was looking for a temporary mate. He said you were doing odd jobs until you moved to Mexico with your folks."

"Julio is a good friend," Tony said gratefully.

"He recommended you highly," Captain Ruiz answered. "My mate gets twenty-five per cent of the day's receipts. But we don't go out every day, of course. Is that all right with you?

"Sure."

"Very well. I'll expect you on the *Albacora* tomorrow morning, about seven. We already have a passenger for tomorrow."

"I'll be there, Captain! Thanks!"

When the man was gone, Tony sat down on the dock again, looking much happier than he had looked for the last three days.

"What a stroke of luck!" he breathed. "Julio *is* a friend. The *Albacora* is first class and gets top prices. If this had happened a couple of months ago, I'd probably have been able to earn the whole amount, by this time."

"It's silly to figure like that," Peter pointed out, in his

common-sense way. "If the captain has a regular mate, you couldn't have. Might as well wish you'd found a fortune in the street. But anyhow, you'll be making some money while we wait for this Puerto Marques thing. And it'll be fun," he added enviously. "Wish I could go out with you."

"After I've been working a day or two, I'll see if I can get the captain to take you sometimes," Tony promised. "And meantime I'll let Armando know he's to get in touch with you, if I'm not home. Or maybe he could paddle out to the mouth of Puerto Marques bay and give me a signal on the *Albacora*. Pedro, I have a feeling that everything is going to work out, after all! Being offered this job right now seems like a good sign!"

"Tony, how would you like to get up here on the flying bridge and see if you can spot a sailfish for Mr. Sutton? I've stared so long my eyes are watering!"

"*Sí, Capitán, con mucho gusto!*"

Passing Peter, who was in the cabin uncapping a Coca-Cola for Mrs. Sutton, Tony said, "You having fun, Pedro? How do you like being a deck hand?"

Peter looked around to see that no one was listening, and answered in a low voice, "I love it, Tony! But I'm getting worried—about time."

"You and me, too! But our chance will come soon, Pedro."

The words echoed in his head as he stationed himself at the controls on the flying bridge and began scanning the too-quiet waters for sign of an emerging sailfish tail or a dark shadow.

He had decided, now, to *make* the chance come soon. He was tired of waiting.

Two whole weeks had passed since the first treasure hunt. Armando had reported faithfully, always with the same bad news that the guard on the Puerto Marques property had not been relaxed. One evening Tony had risked going over to confirm the fact for himself. Time was getting short now, and he was more and more concerned, although he tried to forget it during his working hours.

He loved the job on the *Albacora* and he did it with conscientious thoroughness; taking his turn at the wheel, searching the waters for big fish, baiting the hooks, and in general keeping the fishing clients happy.

He found that he enjoyed working with tourists when there were only two or three of them, all intent on catching fish. It wasn't at all like the glass-bottomed boat venture, when he'd had to make speeches to an audience and put on a rehearsed act. Besides, there was no belligerent Lencho to contend with here. Tony sincerely liked Captain Ruiz and was doubly grateful to him when he good-naturedly allowed Peter to go with them sometimes.

Tony hadn't told Peter yet that he had made up his mind that if nothing happened within the next forty-eight hours, he was going to try somehow to get around that guard himself and do some more digging.

He hated to have Peter involved in a second expedition—which might be even more dangerous than the first one. Yet he didn't see how he could keep it from him, either. Peter was the most loyal friend he had ever had, sticking to him through everything. And Peter would be brokenhearted if he were not allowed to take part in the second treasure hunt—the treasure hunt that would solve all Tony's problems, or end all hope. . . .

"Strangest looking water I've ever seen!"

Tony turned, startled from his worrying thoughts, to see the captain standing behind him, frowning down at the lacquer-smooth sea.

"In the twenty years I've been in the fishing business, I've never seen the water so quiet this far out. Nor the air so still, at this time of day. What do you make of it, Tony?"

"I don't know, sir. It *is* strange. Almost like the calm before a hurricane. But we wouldn't be having a hurricane in January!"

"Not likely." The captain's voice was thoughtful. "But it probably has something to do with the earthquakes. I'll confess I don't like it!"

"There certainly have been a lot of *temblores*," Tony agreed.

"Over a hundred in the last two weeks, the papers report," the captain said grimly. "Of course, most of them have been quite small. Nothing like that jolt fourteen days ago."

Tony was silent, thinking of that long tremor that had frightened off Lencho and his pals. It had been lucky for him that it had happened just then! Nevertheless he, too, wished the small quakes would let up.

"I'd like to go back to port right now," the captain said uneasily. "Partly because of this strange-looking sea, and partly because my wife hasn't been at all well, the last couple of days. But these Suttons are such nice people, and they want a sailfish so bad, I hate to cut the trip short."

Tony nodded. He hated to disappoint the Suttons, too. They were the nicest of all the passengers the *Albacora* had taken fishing in the last two weeks. This was their third trip without even a strike, and although they were cheerful and uncomplaining, they did have their hearts set on catching a big fish.

"Let's try for a little while longer," Tony suggested. "Maybe they'll get one quickly and then we can go back."

"All right, boy. Keep a sharp lookout. Your eyes are younger than mine and they can see farther."

Continuing his watch alone, after the captain had returned to the cabin, Tony thought how fine it would be to work for Ruiz if the treasure hunt yielded enough money to satisfy his uncle, and if the captain didn't already have a regular mate, and if—

Just at that moment he saw it! An enormous black shadow, not far astern.

"It's a big one!" he yelled down, his skin prickling with excitement and his own worries temporarily forgotten. "Behind your bait, Mr. Sutton! Drop your line back! Give him more line!"

The American tensed as he saw the fish strike the moving bait with its bill, and he released enough line to make the big fish think it had stunned its prey. But this fish was wary. It followed the bait for several seconds before it struck again, viciously, knocking the line out of the clothespin on the outrigger.

"Be careful!" Tony called, hardly daring to breathe.

"Wait!" A few seconds later he shouted joyously, "He took it right in! Hook him now—hard! It's a *marlin*—a whopping marlin!"

The captain leaped up the ladder. "I'll take over, Tony. You go down and give him some pointers—if he needs them. Your English is better than mine when I get excited!"

Tony jumped into the cockpit, not bothering with the ladder.

"Put the reel on free-spool and let him have lots of line," he cautioned the American. "This is an awfully big fish for the size tackle you're using, and if the line is tight, it'll break."

Feeling the tension of the hook now, the marlin took off like a streak of lightning. Some distance away it suddenly erupted like Mount Vesuvius, leaping wildly into the air, twisting, writhing and throwing spray as it fell. It was a spectacular and thrilling sight in the afternoon sun.

"The camera, Beth, the camera!" shouted Mr. Sutton.

But before his wife could get the camera in focus, the fish went down. It raced underwater for some distance, to come up far astern and begin jumping toward the boat, two thirds of its great silver-purple body out of the water, leaving a wake of foam behind it.

Tony heard Mrs. Sutton click the camera several times, but he wasn't looking at her. His attention was divided between the acrobatic fish and the reel in Mr. Sutton's hands.

The fish submerged again, then came up, leaping

several feet out of the water. The glittering head shook savagely before it fell back with a resounding crash.

"Man, oh, man, just look at that blue dynamite!" Peter whispered in awe, to nobody in particular.

"It's the biggest marlin I ever saw!" Tony breathed. "A lot bigger than the one Mr. Williams brought in."

Suddenly the fish began to skitter on its tail toward the boat and Mr. Sutton reeled in madly. The captain speeded the motor, to help keep the line taut. Then the marlin raced away at right angles. Finally it bored straight down again, taking practically all the line off the reel.

Mr. Sutton fought valiantly, his eyes bright, his face streaming perspiration. Mrs. Sutton was busy taking pictures. Peter, too, was getting in some shots with the captain's camera, now that he had recovered a little from his first excitement.

"I believe that marlin is over four hundred pounds," the captain called down with satisfaction. "Might set the season's record—if you bring it in."

The caution in his last words seemed prophetic. Five minutes later, when the big fish seemed at last to be tiring a little, and Mr. Sutton had slowly worked it closer to the boat, the marlin unexpectedly came to life, made its most spectacular leap of all—and the line snapped.

"*Caramba!*" the captain exclaimed sadly from above.

"Oh, Bill, you lost it!" Mrs. Sutton's voice was a moan.

Tony took one look at the American, whose face was a picture of tragedy as he numbly held the rod with the broken line dangling in the water. Then Tony peeled off his shirt and soared from the rail in a shallow dive that carried him far out. Catching hold of the floating loose end which was attached to Mr. Sutton's rod, he swam furiously to where the other end was trailing just below the surface.

The marlin, fortunately, was now headed toward the boat, unaware that it was free. So there was no tension on the line as Tony quickly tied the two ends together in a strong knot.

"Now!" he yelled, treading water. "Take up the slack—quick—before he jumps again and throws the hook."

Mr. Sutton, paralyzed with surprise at the speed with which he had lost his fish and recovered it again, obeyed automatically, a big smile gradually dawning on his face.

The captain maneuvered the boat cautiously to help Mr. Sutton and to keep the line from tangling in the propeller.

"Watch it, Tony!" he yelled. "The marlin's headed straight toward you! We'll be back to pick you up!"

Tony struck off at an angle in a fast crawl, out of the path of the oncoming fish and its dangerous, spearlike bill.

The boat pulled away quickly and in a few seconds the line was taut again.

Left alone in the ocean, Tony turned over on his back and floated. The water was warm and still. It was like floating in a quiet pond. He felt very peaceful for a few minutes—as though he would like to stay there forever, lying on the still water, unthinking. . . .

But as he lay looking up at the sky, an eerie orange light seemed to obscure the afternoon sun. There *was* something strange about this day! Something almost ominous. He just hoped that if anything was going to happen, it wouldn't be serious enough to upset his plans for a second visit to Adan's property.

His mind began working over the details again. Actually, it should be easy, this time. Armando could distract the guard. He could say he had heard someone digging far down the lagoon. With the guard off on a wild-goose chase, Tony and Peter would have a clear field. And without Chico's panic hampering the operations, they could dig all night, if they had to.

That first experience had taught him a number of things. *This* time they'd take a bus and go straight to Armando's house, where the tools were already hidden —more efficient tools than they'd had the first time. Then, instead of that torturing walk along the lagoon, they would go by water in Armando's *canoa*. That way they'd arrive at the site fresh and ready for work—not exhausted like the last time.

And *this* time they'd find the old man's treasure. They'd give the government its half, required by law, all honest and legal. It should be easy. There shouldn't be much danger at all, with the guard called off. . . .

His mind absorbed with plans, Tony had almost forgotten about the weather and the marlin by the time the launch returned and slowed down for him. Captain Ruiz had descended from the flying bridge and was now at the controls below.

"Hop aboard, Tony—fast," the captain called. "The marlin's sulking somewhere below and there's no telling what it'll do next."

Peter gave him a hand and Tony scrambled aboard, dripping water. Mr. Sutton looked tired and hot, but he turned a beaming smile on the boy.

"That was fast thinking, Tony—and fast work, tying that line. I'll have you to thank if I catch the biggest fish I've ever even seen!"

"I was glad to have a dip," Tony smiled. "Cooled me off."

"There's an extra pair of pants in the locker," Captain Ruiz said. "Better change."

"Oh, I'll dry in the sun."

"What sun?" the captain murmured in Spanish. And Tony knew that Captain Ruiz, too, had been observing the change in the sky.

The marlin continued its gymnastics, first leaping, then boring down in the deep water, trying desperately to rid itself of the hook. Mr. Sutton alternately pumped in a few hundred feet of line and then lost them back again. He was proving himself an able fisherman, but it promised to be a long-drawn-out battle. The fish was so heavy and full of fight that it had to be worked with the utmost care, in order to avoid breaking the line again.

After another half hour had passed, the water suddenly began to heave with a strange, oily motion. Captain Ruiz and Tony simultaneously looked at the sky.

"Mr. Sutton." The captain's voice was reluctant. "I hate to tell you but I think we'd better cut that line after all, and get back to port. I don't like the look of the weather."

14

The Big Wave

The American stared at him increduously.

"Oh, *no!*" he groaned. "The biggest fish I've seen in my life—on my line for the second time—and you talk about cutting it!"

"It hurts me to do it," Captain Ruiz said sadly, "but it may be another hour or so before you could bring it in. And there's something strange going on. Look at the water. We're evidently having some small submarine earthquakes. I've never seen anything just like this, so I don't know what to expect. I can't let you run into possible danger for a fish, no matter how big it is."

Mr. Sutton looked mournfully at his wife.

"It's a shame, Bill," she said. "You wanted it so much. But of course we ought to do whatever the captain thinks best."

Tony and Peter winced, too, as Captain Ruiz slowly brought out his knife and cut the line which set the big marlin free.

There was no doubt that they should get back. The thirty-four-foot cruiser was now pitching like a peanut shell in the turbulent water.

157

Captain Ruiz gunned the motor and ran full speed toward Acapulco. No one spoke until the boat had entered the bay, where the water was more quiet, although it still acted in a somewhat unpredictable fashion.

The other fishing boats were also returning to port, but instead of trying to dock on the wharf, as usual, they were anchoring out in the bay. Passengers were let down into speedboats and taken to the fishermen's beach in the sheltered curve of the coast.

"That means the water must be pretty choppy along the docks," Tony said to Peter in a low voice as they all watched the proceedings.

Captain Ruiz strained his eyes toward shore, looking concerned.

"I don't like it," he muttered. "I don't like it at all."

As they came a little nearer, they could hear instructions being called over a loud-speaker near the fishing headquarters.

"Stay where you are, *Albacora*, and wait your turn." The voice came thinly over the water. "We'll have your passengers off in a minute."

Captain Ruiz cut the engine, while Tony translated the instructions for the Suttons.

"I guess it's a good thing we came back when we did," he added to Mr. Sutton as they watched the unusual activity on the docks, "but I'm sure sorry about that marlin, sir."

The man gave him a melancholy smile. "You did your best to get it for me, Tony. Oh, well, it was only a fish," he sighed. "But what a fish! Looks as though we're going

to have something else to think about, if these earthquakes keep up."

In about ten minutes a speedboat came zooming out
to the *Albacora,* and the Suttons were taken off.

"What's going on, anyway?" Captain Ruiz asked the
boy in the small boat. "Does anyone know?"

"No, sir, nobody knows for sure. But the water is sure
acting peculiar—" The boy broke off. "Say, you're Captain Ruiz, aren't you? I was told to report to you that
your wife is quite sick. She was taken to the hospital
about two hours ago."

The captain's face paled under the deep sunburn.
"That settles it, then. I was going to stay with the
Albacora—just in case—but now I'm going ashore." He
jumped into the speedboat. "Throw over both anchors,
Tony, and lash down everything you can. You and Pedro
be ready to go ashore on the next trip this boy makes."

Tony shook his head. "I'll stay with the *Albacora,*
Captain," he said quietly. "She's too close in. If this
water keeps churning and she should drag the anchors,
she might get damaged on the docks."

The captain was silent for a moment and then he said
heavily, "This boat is all I have in the world, to make a
living, but I couldn't let you take the risk, Tony. I don't
think anything is likely to happen in this sheltered bay,
but we've never had submarine earthquakes before, so
I don't know. Come on, make everything fast and get
ready to go ashore."

It was an order, but still Tony did not move. His eyes
traveled quickly over the *Albacora.* He hadn't realized

until that moment how much he had come to love the beautiful cruiser, in two short weeks. Even though his job on her would be over, the possibility of having her smashed up on the wharf or on sharp rocks was unbearable to him.

"Captain, let me stay," he pleaded. "Whatever happens, I'll be all right, away from land. You know better than anyone else that the *Albacora* is seaworthy."

Captain Ruiz shook his head, and the boy in the speedboat said impatiently, "Hurry up and decide. I have to get to the other fishing launches as fast as I can."

"Pedro, you go back with them now," Tony spoke quickly. "Your father will be worried about you."

"No, he won't. I'm staying with you," Peter said firmly.

The speedboat runner quickened his motor. "I can't wait all day," he muttered. "We're going now. If you boys want to be taken off later, signal, and I'll come back for you."

"I'll send you back for them," Captain Ruiz said grimly. "Tony—hey, wait a minute!"

But the boat was already gone, zipping its way to the beach while the captain stood in the stern, looking back at the boys with eyes that were half angry and half troubled.

Tony sighed. "You should have gone, Pedro. I'm not going to wait for that boat to come back. Captain Ruiz may be mad at me, but he'll get over it. Somehow I just *can't* leave the *Albacora*, not knowing what might happen to her."

"And I wouldn't let you stay out here alone—for anything," Peter said. "We're twins, remember? We'll be all right. People are just excited because they've never seen anything just like this before."

Tony was inclined to agree with him, but just the same he turned the *Albacora's* nose toward the open sea. If the water should become any rougher, the farther they were from land, the better off they'd be.

They had almost reached the mouth of the bay when they felt themselves suddenly rising high and fast on an *outgoing* surge of sea. Taken by surprise, Tony gripped the wheel more tightly, while Peter seized the binoculars, staring inland.

"Tony!" His voice was awed. "The water's gone out! For about fifty feet out from the docks, you can see the bottom!"

Tony grabbed the glasses and looked. Peter was right. It was a strange sight! Small launches normally rocking in ten to twelve feet of water, were now stranded on the dry bottom of the bay. That meant that the speedboats would be grounded, too—so he and Peter couldn't leave the *Albacora* even if they wanted to.

They could hear excited shouts from people on the dock, and the clamor of bells sounding an alarm.

"Pedro, maybe it's a tidal wave!" Tony said breathlessly. "I remember my father telling about one they had here, when he was a boy. He said the water went *out* from shore, first, and then in a few minutes a big wave came in and flooded the whole lower part of the town!"

"Do you think we should stay here, or get out farther?" Peter asked, his voice shaking a little.

"We should get out," Tony said decisively. "If there's

a really big wave, we don't want to be where it will break on us. It *could* smash this boat to kindling wood! Out farther, we'll probably be able to ride it."

But even as he turned back to the controls to put on speed, he saw it! From beyond the mouth of the bay, a surge of water was approaching with a slow, ominous movement. It didn't come like a breaker but like a huge swell, as though something were pushing it up from below.

"Throw over the bow anchor—quick!" he yelled to Peter.

He himself ran to double the mooring lines on the stern anchor; then, racing back to the wheel, he gripped it with all his strength, holding it steady, with the *Albacora's* nose at a slight angle to the incoming swell. If that surge of sea struck them either broadside or directly head on, there might be nothing left of the *Albacora*—nor of Peter and himself.

"Harness yourself into a fishing chair, Pedro, and hold on for dear life!"

Tony's heart was thundering against his ribs as he watched the thing approach. He couldn't think of it as the familiar sea. It was more like some malevolent force from another world. Fascinated, he stood with his eyes glued on it, prepared to turn the engine to full speed the second that it arrived.

"Here it comes!" he shouted. "Are you all right, Pedro?"

"All right!" Peter's voice was shrill with excitement. "I'm here, holding onto the rail!"

Alarmed because Peter had not made himself more secure, Tony half turned to warn him. But it was too late.

At that moment it came—a great swell that lifted them high into the air. Hanging onto the wheel, Tony felt as though he were soaring on the tail of a kite. It was the strangest sensation he had ever had. The *Albacora* was lifted like a toy.

But what he had said to Captain Ruiz was true: the *Albacora* was one of the few boats in the Acapulco fishing fleet that was built for the open sea. She rode the big wave gallantly. All would have been well, except that as soon as they were pitched down again in the trough of the wave, there was a sudden jerk of a backward undertow, so sharp and unexpected that the *Albacora* lurched violently, and Peter was taken by surprise. His tight grip on the rail had unconsciously relaxed after the wave had passed, and now he was jolted loose and hurled against the stern. His head struck with a sharp crack, and a second later he had toppled overboard.

Hearing the thud, Tony turned just in time to see his friend go over and disappear into the heaving water. For a second, he stood paralyzed with horror. Then, with frantic haste, he secured another mooring rope to the stern, tossed the loose end overboard, tore off his shirt in a single movement and dived straight down where Peter had disappeared.

Ordinarily, it would not have been too difficult to find him, for the water below the surface is usually calm, even during a wind storm. But now, due to the submarine earthquakes, it was full of currents that raised clouds of sand and foam.

Tony drove down as far and as fast as he could, his

ears roaring with the pressure. Plowing back and forth under the water, he tried to search as calmly and thoroughly as possible, but his mind was clouded with sick anxiety. He knew that if Peter had been knocked unconscious by the blow on his head, there was no hope for him. The boy's lungs would fill with water immediately, and he would be drowned by this time. Tony could only pray that the thud had sounded worse than it was, and that Peter had been conscious and breathing when he hit the water.

Tony stayed under until his lungs were agonized for air and then he surfaced, gasping, to take his bearings. The *Albacora* was a good fifty feet away now. It was hard to tell whether she was dragging her anchors, or whether Tony himself had been more buffeted by the currents than he realized.

Pumping his lungs with air, he went down again, swimming underwater in the direction of the boat but going deeper than before. He felt the pressure surges on his ears and the fleeting thought crossed his mind that he had been forbidden to dive. But it didn't matter now—whether he got a recurrence of the bends, or whether he drowned, looking for Peter.

He knew only one thing with absolute certainty: he had no intention of going back to Acapulco alone, without his young American friend.

The second trip under proved as fruitless as the first. Coming up for air again, he was surprised to find that the water was now quite calm. Suddenly, as he scanned the surface, not far away he saw a yellow blob of something. Even as he strained his eyes, his heart leaping with hope, it disappeared.

Somehow certain that what he had seen was Peter's blond head, Tony swam furiously on the surface for a few feet until he was sure that his sense of direction would carry him straight. Then he clawed his way under and submarined down, his mind carefully calculating the angle where he might hope to intercept Peter—if it *was* Peter's head that he had seen.

For seconds that seemed hours, his threshing hands contacted nothing. Then, abruptly, his right hand brushed against a soft object. An instant later, with an inner shout of thanksgiving, he had a firm grip on Peter's arm.

Kicking madly, he swam surfaceward. With one hand under Peter's chin, he forced his winded body into the fastest sprint he had ever demanded of it, toward the *Albacora*.

Treading water behind the boat, he swiftly tied the loose line he had thrown overboard under Peter's armpits. Then, scrambling aboard himself on the anchor rope, he pulled the inert body of the blond boy after him.

Every muscle in Tony's body ached, but he was unaware of it. Kneeling in front of Peter, he used the method of artificial respiration which he had learned from the lifeguards on the beach, that of supplementing direct pressure on the lungs with indirect pressure created by rhythmically moving the boy's arms. Thus the cycle was continuous. As he rocked back after pressing on Peter's lungs, he lifted his friend's arms and brought them forward and upward.

Forward and upward, backward and down. Up—down —up—down. Tony worked like a robot, trying to ignore his numbing fear that it would be of no use—that Peter had been under too long. He clamped down on his teeth which were chattering with strain and nervous exhaustion.

Forward and upward. Backward and down. . . .

And at last he was rewarded! Peter's lungs began to take on a faint, ragged rhythm of their own, and his eyelids fluttered almost imperceptibly. Tony restrained an impulse to shout aloud with joy. Instead, he clamped his teeth tighter and continued his exertions until finally the blond boy's breathing hung on more steadily.

Suddenly, salt water gushed from Peter's nose and mouth. He half turned over, groaning and retching. Then he lay back and the blue eyes opened.

Tony leaned against one of the fishing chairs, his weariness washed away in overwhelming relief.

"You're all right, Pedro!" he shouted happily. "You're going to be okay!"

Peter nodded, smiling faintly.

After they had both rested for a few minutes, Tony helped Peter up and put him on one of the cabin bunks, covering him with an old sweater of the captain's which had been left hanging in the locker. Then he searched the tiny galley and was delighted to find half a jar of instant coffee. Heating water on the gasoline stove, he poured it over most of the coffee, and holding Peter's head up, he made him sip it hot and strong.

"Wow!" Peter's voice was almost normal. "That burned my tongue, but it was like a shot in the arm!"

Tony grinned. "You're tough, Pedro! You're tougher than I thought!"

He fixed coffee for himself and felt new life flowing through his veins as he downed it. Then he rummaged around until he found a towel and extra shorts for them both. In dry clothes and fortified with a second cup of coffee, Peter sat up in the bunk, still weak and dazed but looking more like himself every minute.

"You saved my life, Tony," he said quietly.

"Well, I couldn't very well go back to Acapulco and tell your father I'd thrown you overboard!" Tony grinned, trying to lighten the serious moment.

"He wouldn't believe you if you did," Peter said soberly. "You know he thinks a lot of you."

"I can't imagine why he should," Tony said ruefully. "I'm always getting you into trouble. But this was the worst!"

"You've never gotten me into anything that you haven't gotten me out of," Peter said. He paused and leaned back, closing his eyes for a moment.

"Don't talk, Pedro," Tony urged. "Rest for a while. That was quite a ducking you had!"

Peter smiled at the understatement. "I don't need to rest my voice," he said, "and I want to tell you something, Tony. You said just now that I'm tougher than you thought. Well, I am. I'm a lot tougher than I was three months ago, and it's because of the outdoor life I've had with you. You see, I had rheumatic fever when I was small, and Dad was afraid I was always going to be sickly. He wants, more than anything, for me to be strong and healthy. So he's grateful to you, see? I didn't tell you before because I hate to talk about sickness. I don't like to think about it."

Tony looked at him thoughtfully. "You know, you *are* filling out, Pedro. You look like a different boy—except that you're a little pale at the moment!"

It had happened so gradually that he hadn't really noticed it until just then. Peter *had* put on weight and his arms, shoulders and legs were well muscled now. His face looked more mature. Burned black from the sun, he looked like any Acapulco boy, except for the startlingly blue eyes and the sun-bleached hair.

"I kind of wondered why your father was so willing to let you go along with me on all these things we've been doing," Tony said. "That explains it."

Peter nodded. "He's urged me on—not that I needed any urging!" He grinned but sobered quickly. "This accident—it was my own darned carelessness," he said contritely. "You told me what to do but I thought I'd be all right, holding tight to the rail. I didn't want to miss anything! I stayed on the boat to try to help you, and I just made you more trouble."

"Well, it really wasn't your fault, Pedro. You haven't had too much experience yet, with the sea and with boats. I was to blame for not making sure you were safe. Now lie down for a while and take it easy. I want you to be completely over this before your father sees you!"

15

The Last Hope

AS PETER OBEDIENTLY LAY BACK ON THE BUNK, CLOSING his eyes, Tony felt depression closing over him again. This was just another one of his long list of mistakes, he thought dismally—letting Peter almost get drowned. Between his own bungling and the impersonal jinx that seemed to pursue him, everything he touched went wrong!

It shook his confidence all over again, filling him with new apprehension about the treasure hunting. Was bad luck going to follow him to the very end?

One thing was sure, now. He would have to keep Peter out of the second expedition to Puerto Marques. After this close brush with death, Tony didn't intend to expose him to any more danger, if he could help it. He and Armando would have to find some third boy who could be trusted. There had to be at least three. One to distract the guard and two to do the digging. . . .

"Ahoy, *Albacora!*"

The shout made Tony jump. He was so absorbed in his thoughts that he had neither seen nor heard the speedboat approaching. It was not the one that had carried the

Suttons and Captain Ruiz to the beach. This one was run by a boy whom Tony knew slightly.

"*Hola*, Manuel," he called back.

"Well, Tony! I didn't know you were on the *Albacora!* Are you all right? The port captain has been watching the bay and all the boats that were out, through binoculars. He thought he saw someone go overboard and he sent me to check on you first."

"All present and accounted for—now." Tony glanced at Peter, who had opened his eyes again, and heaved an inner sigh of relief that he could give that answer. Then he added curiously, "How did you manage to get out here? I thought most of the small boats—"

"You thought right," Manuel said grimly. "Most of them are banged up, one way or another. But mine happened to be high and dry, because I painted it yesterday. When they asked for volunteers, in the fishing office, I offered to help, but it took a while to get the boat in the water and get the motor working."

"Is there a lot of damage on shore?" Tony asked.

"Quite a bit. But no people seriously hurt—that we know of. Two boats are still missing. If you're really okay, do you want to help me hunt them? How's your gasoline?"

Tony checked. There was plenty of fuel, but he hesitated before calling back an answer.

"How do you feel, Pedro?" he asked in a low voice. "We really should get back to shore, after all you've been through."

"I'm fine," Peter said stoutly. "Only one thing wrong

with me—I'm hungry! That ducking, and then losing my lunch, made me awfully empty."

Tony grinned a little. "Well, that's easy to remedy. There's plenty of food left from the Suttons' box lunches. Just the same, I think we ought to go back, now that the water's normal again."

"What do you say?" Manuel called up. "I told them on shore that I'd bring you straight back, if anything was wrong with you or the boat. Otherwise, I was to ask you to help search, since you're already out here."

Tony looked again at Peter, who nodded.

"All right, then," he called back. "Where do you want us to go? What boats are missing?"

"One's a private sailboat from the Yacht Club," Manuel answered. "The other is the *Pelicano*—a glass-bottomed boat that works out of Caleta Beach. Something odd about that: it's been missing since late yesterday afternoon, and the owner, Captain García, thinks it may have been stolen, instead of holed up on account of weather. It was last seen around sundown, heading east in the direction of Puerto Marques and the Costa Chica."

Peter sat up suddenly and he and Tony stared at each other, their minds meeting in a single thought.

"The *Pelicano!* Puerto Marques!" Tony's voice was stupefied. "Pedro, Lencho's beat us to it!"

"Looks like he's trying," Peter said. "We can't let him get away with that!"

Tony set his jaw tightly. "Your launch is faster," he yelled down to Manuel. "You look for the sailboat. It's probably around by the Quebrada and it's more likely to be in serious trouble. We'll go after the *Pelicano*. I have an idea I know where it is!"

"Okay! If anything happens and you need help, send up a flare!"

The speedboat raced away and Tony ran to pull in the anchors. His face was rigid and his hands were trembling with anger.

"If Lencho has found that treasure and made off with it," he muttered savagely, "I'll follow him and beat him to a pulp, no matter where he's gone!"

"I never thought *he'd* try again," Peter said. "I thought he was too scared—like Chico."

"So did I. I just counted him out completely after that earthquake scare. But I should have known his greed would get the better of his fright. He's tougher and more persistent than Chico."

Another mistake I made, Tony thought, underrating Lencho's nerve.

The two boys were silent as Tony ran the *Albacora* at full speed toward Puerto Marques. Peter was wolfing down the leftover sandwiches nervously, as though to give himself strength for whatever might come. Tony was too angry, now, to feel either hunger or weariness. If Lencho had cheated him out of his last chance—!

They had barely entered the mouth of Puerto Marques Bay when they saw a *canoa* coming out to meet them. The boy in it half stood, gesturing with his paddle.

Tony killed the motor of the *Albacora*. "It's Armando," he said, "signaling us to stay here."

The two boys waited impatiently while Armando

covered the distance between them with swift, expert strokes.

"What's happened?" Tony called sharply as the dugout approached. "Lencho's been here, hasn't he?"

"Yes." Armando wiped the perspiration from his face with the back of his hand. "But he's not the only one! Throw me a line and help me aboard. I've got a lot to tell you."

With the *canoa* tied, Tony and Peter pulled Armando into the cockpit and he sat down in one of the fishing chairs.

"It's all up, Tony. But not on account of Lencho, though he was going to try!"

"Who, then?" Tony demanded angrily. "Chico?"

Armando shook his head. "Let me start at the beginning. Yesterday morning a real sharp-looking car—a Cadillac—came into the village, driven by a middle-aged, well-dressed man who went at once to see the *alcalde*. I had a hunch—and I hung around, keeping my eyes and ears open. It wasn't long before the whole village knew that the man was old Adan's nephew, from Chihuahua, and that he had papers proving his right to all of Adan's property! In fact, he was the one who had the guard put on the place. He had telegraphed the *alcalde*, more than two weeks ago."

"Adan mentioned a nephew to Chico," Tony whispered numbly. "But he was sure he was dead."

"Well, he isn't." Armando's voice was grim. "He's very much alive and his name is Don Guillermo Robles. He's definitely established his claim on the property. I heard him tell the *alcalde* that he might do some excavating but that he didn't think they'd find a thing in the way of treasure."

"Why? How does he know?" Peter broke in.

"He believes," Armando said slowly, "that his Uncle Adan had delusions about that treasure. Because his own father—Adan's brother—looked for it years ago, before he ever moved to Chihuahua, and he never found anything. Don Guillermo's going to extend the coconut plantation back onto that strip of land. Says there's always a good market for copra. He's a hardheaded businessman—not a dreamer, like Adan."

"And like me," Tony said bitterly.

"I wouldn't say you were exactly a dreamer, Tony."

"Not always, maybe." Tony stared down at the deck. "But in this case—I think I knew all along, deep down, that we were chasing a dream. Yet I kept on. I got 'treasure fever'—like you said, Pedro."

Peter changed the subject, trying to distract Tony from his disappointment. "When did Lencho come?" he asked Armando.

"Yesterday afternoon. When he found Don Guillermo already here, looking over his land, he was wild!"

"What did he do?" Peter asked, as Tony remained silent.

Armando shrugged. "What could he do? He stayed till this afternoon, to make sure there was absolutely no hope, and by that time the water was churning up, so he left the *Pelicano* here and took a bus back to Acapulco."

Tony looked up dully. "Where *is* the *Pelicano*? I don't

see it in the cove. We're supposed to be searching for it. That's how we happened to come over here."

"Lencho got some natives to help him pull it up on the beach when the water began to rough up, and it was lucky he did. We didn't get much of that tidal wave— Puerto Marques is too landlocked. But the water rose, just the same."

"Well, I'll tell Captain García that his boat's here," Tony muttered, "but I'll let Lencho explain how it got here."

"He's going to have quite a bit to explain," Armando said. "He looked really beat when he left here—and I doubt that he'll bother you from now on, Tony."

Tony shrugged. The feud between himself and Lencho no longer mattered. He'd be leaving Acapulco in a few days, anyway, he thought with despair.

"Well, we better get back," he said, "or they'll be sending out another boat to look for us."

"I was going to come to Acapulco tonight, to tell you what happened. Since you came over, I won't have to."

Armando hauled on the rope, pulling the *canoa* close to the *Albacora*. Tony and Peter held it while he jumped in.

"I'm awfully sorry, Tony, that things didn't work out —for all of us."

Tony nodded without speaking and waved good-by. He watched Armando pulling away toward the beach with rapid strokes, and then went to start the engine of the *Albacora*.

"It's all over, Pedro," he said lifelessly. "This is the

end. Everything I've been connected with for the last three months has gone wrong. I've failed."

"Don't say that, Tony." Peter tried to be heartening, but his eyes were clouded with distress. "You didn't fail. It was just—circumstances."

Tony stood at the wheel in moody silence for a while.

"I believe the whole trouble, Pedro, is the money part," he said sadly. "It seems to me that as soon as a person begins to work *only* for money—with a kind of desperation—then things are bound to get twisted. I wouldn't have had anything to do with this treasure hunting, if Uncle Juan hadn't insisted on my raising money fast. I really felt guilty about it, all along."

He paused and then said something which he believed profoundly, with all his heart, *"The real treasure of Acapulco isn't buried gold, Pedro.* It's the place itself— partly the beauty the tourists rave about, but even more, for me, a certain way of life."

Peter nodded, understanding perfectly.

"It seems it isn't enough, though," Tony went on, almost in a whisper, "to love a place so much that you'd rather starve than leave it. . . ."

His voice trailed off as he thought of the many things he loved: the pearl-colored dawns . . . the beat of the hot sun on his skin and the cool sting of salt water . . . diving through the fairyland jungles under the surface . . . the low-hanging, orange tropical moons . . . the solitude of the night fishing . . . or the long days like those he had spent on the *Albacora*, hunting the big game fish. . . .

He realized that his eyes were wet and he ran the back

of his hand over them, ashamed. It was bad enough to have to leave all this. He didn't have to cry like a baby about it!

With a quick side glance, he saw that Peter was not looking at him. The troubled blue eyes were fixed pensively on the open ocean.

Tony ran the *Albacora* at low speed. He was in no hurry to get back to Acapulco. He knew that now there was no escape from the prospect that had haunted him these last three months: visions of that chilly, nerve-racking, labyrinthian city of four and a half million struggling humans . . . himself, in a bellboy's uniform, jumping to the sound of a desk clerk's clanging bell . . . the hotel school at night: a different kind of school, more severe and exacting than any he'd known before, where he would have to learn the thousand tedious details of dealing with a long succession of tourists.

The thought of it made him physically ill. And he somehow knew, with a strong and terrible conviction, that once he got into it, there would be no escape—ever.

Escape. The word lingered in his mind. *What if he did just that—right now—while he still had a chance?*

What if he landed Peter on Roqueta Island, where he could easily get transportation back to the mainland, while he, Tony, ran the *Albacora* up the coast to a town far enough away so that he wouldn't be known? He could get someone to return the cruiser to its owner, while he hid out for a while, until his uncle's family gave him up and left for Mexico City without him. There were lots of places where he could make a living, fishing and skin diving.

No one would ever find him. He could disappear completely, staying for a time in small villages like Papanoa and Petatlan, and then going on later to Zihuatanejo. Those places were always warm, their waters always teeming with fish. He could live forever in bathing trunks. He could eat sea food, selling enough of it to the villagers to buy a few tortillas and beans.

Eventually, he might go on to Manzanillo and Mazatlán and get work on freighters, in order to buy a small boat of his own.

Or he could go *down* the coast—along the Costa Chica —where the towns were even fewer and more inaccessible. There were places there, he had heard, that were like indescribable dream worlds: fabulously beautiful and untouched small bays; isolated, powder-white beaches where no one had walked before; unfrequented waters that would be a skin diver's paradise.

The people of the villages just inland on the Costa Chica were not sea people. They didn't know what wealth lay at their doorstep. They were farmers, earning a scrubby living from corn patches, raising a few chickens and pigs. A skin diver who worked the Costa Chica could eventually get rich, if he wanted to. And when he was not diving, he could roam in virgin jungle where the trees still harbored chattering monkeys and rare, multicolored birds, or climb the rocky cliffs of mountains that rose straight out of the blue, blue sea.

Tony's fingers tightened on the wheel as he struggled with the temptation. There was nothing impossible about the plan. It could be done.

But he knew, sorrowfully, that *he* couldn't do it. Right

or wrong, Uncle Juan had tried to be good to him and to his sister Marta. He just couldn't do a sneaky thing now, like running away and hiding. And certainly he had no right to borrow the *Albacora*, even for a couple of days.

"Tony, what *are* you going to do?" Peter's voice broke in, sounding as though he had been following Tony's thoughts all the way.

"The only thing there is to do." Tony tried to keep his voice steady. "Go back to Acapulco and face up to the future as well as I can."

16

Insurance for the Future

NEITHER BOY SPOKE AS TONY RAN THE *Albacora* INTO the bay. Nearing the docks, they could see the damage done by the tidal wave: some of the small boats were smashed beyond repair, and debris of various kinds covered the narrow park which separated the wharf from the coast boulevard.

It seemed to Tony as though a week had passed since they had started out in the morning, on a routine fishing trip. After all their harrowing experiences of the past few hours, he rather expected that several people would be on the dock to meet them. But as he anchored the boat and threw the mooring line ashore, the only person who appeared to be waiting for the *Albacora* was Julio.

The older boy wrung their hands after they had jumped out onto the dock.

"Welcome to Acapulco!" he shouted, his homely face splitting in an ear-to-ear grin. "You boys have sure been gone a long time! *Caramba*, it's nice to see you again!"

Peter grinned back weakly, but for once Tony found himself unable to respond to his friend's good humor. Julio knew that Tony's days in Acapulco were numbered, and although he didn't know about the fiasco of the treasure hunting, still he should have guessed that the tidal wave, alone, would be the last straw. It wasn't anything to joke and grin about, Tony thought resentfully.

Then he saw Peter's father coming toward them from the fishing headquarters.

"Well, Pete!" Mr. Carson put his hands on his son's shoulders and held him off for inspection. "You look a little done in, but not too bad—under the circumstances."

Did he know that Peter had almost drowned? Tony wondered.

Mr. Carson answered the unspoken question. "Thanks, Tony," he said in a voice that was rather unsteady, "for bringing Peter back—alive."

"I—wouldn't have come back without him," Tony said, embarrassed. "Did the port captain tell you?"

"He told Julio and I heard. We both got here about the same time—just after that boy, Manuel, had left here to check up on you. I wouldn't care to go through again what I went through until I saw you start out to look for the missing boats. I knew, then, that Pete was absolutely okay, or you wouldn't have gone."

Tony looked down at his feet, embarrassed by the gratitude and confidence implied in Mr. Carson's words.

Julio broke in lightly, ignoring the emotion-charged atmosphere. "I take it you found the *Pelicano*, by the way. Captain García caught up with Lencho, a little while ago, and I believe your former enemy is on his way to jail again, for borrowing a boat without permission."

Tony shrugged. "Then I won't have to report on that."

"No. And now that everything's taken care of, Tony, your uncle wants you. He was here a while ago, and when he found out you were safe, he left, asking me to tell you that he wants to see you right away."

"I thought he would," Tony sighed, gloomy again. "After what happened today, I suppose he's already packing to leave Acapulco."

"I suppose so," Julio agreed, with what seemed to Tony complete heartlessness.

"And Captain Ruiz?"

"He came tearing back to the docks as soon as he heard about the tidal wave, though he didn't know till he got here that you boys were still on the *Albacora*. He had ordered the speedboat to go back for you, when he came ashore, and he had left for the hospital before that first outgoing wave stranded the small boats."

"Was he angry with us for staying aboard?" Tony asked. "There wasn't any way to get back, after the thing started."

"I wouldn't say he was angry—exactly," Julio said in a noncommittal voice. "After Manuel signaled that you were all right, he talked to your uncle for a few minutes and then he went back to the hospital. His wife had an emergency operation, early this afternoon, but she's going to be okay."

"That's good," Tony muttered, thinking that at least *one* thing had gone right today. He wondered what Captain Ruiz and his uncle had been discussing together—probably his own carelessness in letting Peter fall overboard, he thought glumly. They would know about it, of course. Apparently everyone knew.

"Well, let's go now," Julio said briskly. "I promised to deliver you at home."

"We'll all go," Mr. Carson suggested. "Your aunt has invited us to supper, Tony. Sort of a farewell party."

Tony's heart numbed with despair at the word "farewell." He had nothing to say as the four of them crossed the ravaged park and boulevard and climbed the cement steps that led to Tony's house.

Only Julio was voluble, chattering on about the earthquakes and the tidal wave. There had been quite a lot of damage done, he said, but no lives lost and no one even seriously hurt. The restaurant where he worked had been spared, although a few chairs and tables left on the beach had been washed away. As a matter of fact, he went on, Acapulco had gotten off lightly, considering everything. Mexico City and the towns in-between had been harder hit by the quakes.

Tony hardly heard him. He was thinking rather bitterly that Julio was far more insensitive than he had always believed him to be. Even though he owed much to his Caletilla friend, Tony felt that he could never quite forgive him for being so indifferent to his impending exile from Acapulco.

As they entered the patio of the house, Tony saw that his Aunt Raquel was on the veranda, packing a box, and his heart sank still lower. She paused in her work to look at him with a strange, half-sad smile that the boy could not interpret.

All she said was, "I'm glad you're back, my son. Go to your uncle now. He wants to see you alone in his office."

It was just like three months ago, Tony thought, as

his feet dragged unwillingly across the patio to the small office. Then he had sensed that bad news was coming. Now he knew it.

But three months ago there had been an alternative—a reprieve. Now the reprieve had run out.

He stood in the doorway, as he had stood then, watching his uncle work on a ledger. The thin face was paler than usual, and the amber-colored eyes were sober as he looked up.

"Come in, Antonio, and close the door."

Tony obeyed and sat down, his face wooden with the effort to mask his feelings.

For what seemed a long time, Uncle Juan said nothing at all. He sat with his eyes fixed on the pencil he was rolling in his fingers.

Well, go on, get it over with! Tony thought bitterly. I've failed. I'm a beach bum. So now I go to Mexico City to be a bellboy. . . .

When Uncle Juan finally spoke, his voice was quiet. "You think I've been ignoring you all these three months, Tony. Outwardly, I have, but actually I've been following your activities with the closest attention."

Tony slumped lower in his chair. This was even worse than he had expected. Not only had he failed—but Uncle Juan had watched him do it, and he was now going to lecture him about it.

"First you lost the glass-bottomed boat job," his uncle went on. "After that, I knew of your skin-diving efforts, and that you finally got the bends from going too deep."

"Not from going too deep," Tony interrupted desperately. "From coming up too fast, because my air ran out."

He didn't mention the shark. Perhaps Uncle Juan hadn't heard about that.

His uncle held up his hand, as though to halt further self-defense. "I know all about it. The shark, too. Then the night fishing. You *did* find out that there isn't much money in that, didn't you, Antonio? Just as I told you."

"There's enough to live on," Tony said stubbornly, "on a year-round average. But there's not enough to save a lot in a hurry, the way you wanted me to."

His uncle nodded slightly. "After that," he continued, "the treasure hunting at Puerto Marques. That was almost cheating, Tony. You were supposed to earn this money by your own efforts."

"I would have earned it, all right," Tony said grimly, "if we had gotten it. That was one of the worse nights I ever lived through."

An odd expression crossed Uncle Juan's face that Tony would almost have thought was a smile, if he hadn't known that such a thing was impossible. At least, he thought, his uncle didn't know that he had planned to try again—and there was no need to tell him now.

"Well, then finally the deep-sea fishing and this crisis today," his uncle went on inexorably, "which will probably hurt the tourist business for some time. Can you say that any of your efforts have had spectacular success, Tony?"

"No," the boy muttered, looking down at his bare toes. Why did his uncle have to drag it out and rub it in?

he thought wearily. Wasn't it bad enough without that? Uncle Juan had never been a gentle person, but this was the first time that Tony had thought of him as being deliberately cruel.

"You didn't materially succeed at any of it, and you made a lot of mistakes," his uncle repeated. Then, to Tony's astonishment, he added slowly, "But you tried, Antonio. You tried very hard. And, in a way, you succeeded."

Tony stared, dumfounded.

"Somewhere along the line, you made a lot of friends." Uncle Juan's voice was thoughtful. "Some enemies, too, of course, but among the worthwhile people, you made real friends. One after another, in these weeks, they have come to me on your behalf. Captain García came over a month ago, to ask you to work on another of his glass-bottomed boats. He did not hold you responsible for the fight, and he had intervened with the authorities to get you back in their good graces."

Tony opened his mouth to speak and then closed it again.

"Your friend Julio came to propose that you help in his restaurant until you had the necessary stake to buy a boat of your own—but that would have taken years, I think. After that, Don Clemente came to ask me if you could work permanently as his night fishing partner. He said you were a good fisherman and you sold the fish for a higher price than he could get. Also, he appreciated your looking after him while he was ill."

Uncle Juan paused and glanced at Tony, whose mouth was openly gaping now.

"I refused all of these people, or at least I put them off," he continued slowly. "None of these propositions would have given you much security. Moreover, I wanted to observe your own unaided efforts to the end. You know, Tony, that most of all I wanted security for you, and that is why I insisted on the hotel business. But gradually I have come to see, during these weeks, that there are different kinds of security. My kind has always been money."

He gave a faint sigh. "Now, however, two things have convinced me that money isn't necessarily the only insurance for the future. One thing is—I've had word that our hotel in Mexico City was badly damaged by the earthquake two weeks ago."

Tony could only gasp. Words had completely failed him.

"Oh, it's insured, fortunately," his uncle added, "and I'm leaving for the capital in the morning, to see about the repair work. Nevertheless, the damage made me realize that disaster can strike anywhere, anytime, and that money is not always proof against it.

"Apart from that, I have come to see that friends are a kind of security, too. I know now that you would never need to go begging in Acapulco, Tony. In spite of your failures and accidents, you have made a place for yourself here, and I'm beginning to be convinced that it is wrong for me to force you into another environment, doing work that would obviously be distasteful to you."

Tony's heart had begun to boom like a high surf. He was sitting on the edge of his chair now, his mouth still open and his eyes blazing with excitement.

"Tell me, Antonio," his uncle said abruptly, "just how much have you managed to save in the last three months?"

Tony gulped and swallowed and finally found his tongue. "One thousand and forty pesos and sixty centavos," he said breathlessly. He knew to the last penny. He had counted it often enough!

"Bring it here," his uncle ordered.

Tony flew to retrieve it from behind a loose adobe brick in the kitchen. When he returned, his uncle was writing a check. In a moment, he tore it out and handed it to his nephew.

"Here is a check for one thousand, nine hundred and fifty-nine pesos and forty centavos," he said, his face unsmiling. "It is my contribution to your future, Antonio. Captain Ruiz will be here soon, and you can deliver to him your savings and this check, totaling three thousand pesos, which will be a small down payment, giving you an interest in the *Albacora*."

Tony's knees began to feel rubbery and he sat down abruptly as his uncle went on, "The captain and I discussed this when we were both down on the docks, after being reassured that you and young Pedro were all right. Captain Ruiz wants to take you on as mate and part owner of his boat, since his former mate has decided to stay in Chilpancingo and work for the government. He is grateful to you for saving the *Albacora*. Moreover, he, too, likes you and finds you an alert, responsible worker. This was the most promising of the various propositions that have been made, so I agreed. I trust it is in line with your own desires."

It was too sudden. Tony couldn't take it in. He sat glued to the chair, his black eyes fixed unbelievingly on his uncle.

"This doesn't mean that your efforts are over," Uncle Juan warned. "You'll have to work long, hard hours, and save every centavo to meet the monthly payments which you'll owe—for months, or even years."

"I'll work like a slave," Tony breathed. "I'll do any-thing—*anything!*"

Uncle Juan smiled at last, rather sadly.

"You're a good boy, Tony. It hurts a little to have you so happy to part with the only family you have."

Tony jerked his head up. "It isn't that, Uncle Juan!" he protested truthfully. "It's that I couldn't part with Acapulco—and the life I love here."

"I know." His uncle rose. "Well, that's settled, then. Let's go out now and you can tell your friends that they've succeeded in their project of saving Tony for the sea!" He smiled ruefully. "Oh, yes—one other thing. Pedro's father, apparently another devoted friend of yours, has decided to leave the pension where they've been staying, and move into a small house so they can fix their own food. He wants you to live with them. This makes me feel somewhat easier about leaving you here— when the rest of the family joins me in Mexico City, you'll be with a responsible older person."

All of a sudden, Tony began to really believe this miracle that had happened to him, and he exploded into action. First, he crossed the few feet that separated them and pounded his uncle's back—a thing he had never in his life dreamed of doing. Then he ran out the door.

"Pedro—Julio—Marta—Aunt Raquel! I'm staying!" he shouted, insane with joy.

He saw from their faces that they already knew, all except Peter.

"Welcome to Acapulco!" Julio yelled, repeating the words he had said on the dock. And now Tony realized their significance and knew why Julio had seemed so unfeelingly cheerful. He had known then that Tony was staying.

Aunt Raquel gave him the same half-sad smile that she had given him when he came in. "I'm glad for you, Tony," she said. "I was certain from the beginning that we should not take you away from here. But I'll miss you, boy."

"I'll miss you, too," Tony said, feeling a pang as he realized that he would, indeed, miss all of his adopted family, as well as his own sister Marta. "But I'll visit you as often as I can—I promise."

They were all there at the farewell party, which was a farewell only to Uncle Juan who was leaving the following day to attend to the repairs of the Mexico City hotel. Peter and his father, Julio, Don Clemente and Captain Ruiz joined the family party. The latter ate quickly in his haste to get back to his wife at the hospital. But he took time to seal his contract with Tony, giving the boy part interest in the *Albacora*, subject to monthly payments.

"Does the mate and part owner have anything to say about the hiring of deck hands?" Tony asked the captain hopefully, after their business had been concluded.

"He certainly has a vote in it." The captain's eyes

twinkled. "I know what you're thinking. Yes, it's all right with me if Pedro continues to work with us."

"But only on weekends until school lets out," Mr. Carson said firmly. "And *you're* going to finish your schooling in the evenings, Tony. Pete can help you."

Tony nodded, willing to agree to anything now.

"I can see I'm leaving you in good hands," Uncle Juan said. "More than one pair of good hands," he added, bowing to Captain Ruiz.

The captain smiled and returned the bow. Then he turned to Tony. "I must get back to the hospital now. I'll see you on the *Albacora* tomorrow, mate, bright and early."

"I'll spend the night on her, *mi Capitán!*" Tony answered eagerly. "Just to be sure that nothing more happens to *our* boat!"

"And I'll stay with you! May I, Dad?" Peter begged his father.

"If you promise not to fall overboard," Mr. Carson said gravely. "I don't think I could stand that twice."

"I'll try to take much better care of him from now on," Tony said, looking at his blond friend with deep affection.

There was no doubt in his mind that without Peter's constant encouragement and help, his dreams would never, never have come true.

E3